1961- Space ⟨  ⟩
Atlantic Ocea                                        ⟩
accident. But w

When Navy SEALs Dane Maddock and "Bones" Bonebrake are called upon to find the Liberty Bell 7 and recover its secret cargo, they find themselves caught up in a conspiracy from the Cold War era, and only they stand in the way of a powerful man bent on vengeance. Dane and Bones are back in another "Origins" adventure. Sunken ships, deadly creatures, dangerous enemies, mysteries from the past, and all the thrills your heart can stand await you in *Splashdown!*

## PRAISE FOR SPLASHDOWN

*"Wood and Chesler make one powerhouse team! Just when you thought Dane and Bones just couldn't get any better, Rick Chesler comes on board for one tidal wave of a thrilling adventure. Sunken galleons, giant sea creatures, and one heck of a mystery makes Splashdown one book you won't put down 'til the very end." -* **J. Kent Holloway, author of The Dirge of Briarsnare Marsh and Primal Thirst.**

## PRAISE FOR THE DANE MADDOCK ADVENTURES

"Dane and Bones.... Together they're unstoppable. Rip-roaring action from start to finish. Wit and humor throughout. Just one question - how soon until the next one? Because I can't wait."- Graham Brown, author of Shadows of the Midnight Sun

"A story that thrills and makes one think beyond the boundaries of mere fiction and enter the world of 'why not'?"–David Lynn Golemon, Author of CARPATHIAN

"A twisty tale of adventure and intrigue that never lets up and never lets go!" –Robert Masello, author of BESTIARY

"A page-turning yarn with high action, Biblical speculation, ancient secrets, and nasty creatures. Indiana Jones better watch his back!"–Jeremy Robinson, author of SECONDWORLD

"Let there be no confusion: David Wood is the next Clive Cussler.."–Edward G. Talbot, author of 2010: THE FIFTH WORLD

"Hits all the marks that a blockbuster should. Rick Jones, Author of THE CRYPTS OF EDEN

"Flooded with action!"-Rick Chesler, author of BLOOD HARBOR

"Books don't burn hotter than this!"- Steven Savile, author of the Ogmios thrillers.

"Packs in the fist fights, cipher cracking and ancient secrets that all action adventure lovers will enjoy."- J.F. Penn, author of the ARKANE thrillers

# SPLASHDOWN

## A DANE AND BONES ORIGINS STORY

# DAVID WOOD
## RICK CHESLER

Gryphonwood

# Gryphonwood Press

SPLASHDOWN- A DANE AND BONES ORIGINS
STORY.

Published by Gryphonwood Press
www.gryphonwoodpress.com

ISBN-10: 1940095174
ISBN-13: 978-1-940095-17-2

Printed in the United States of America
First printing: April, 2014

# BOOKS BY DAVID WOOD

# BOOKS BY RICK CHESLER

**Tara Shores Thrillers**
Wired Kingdom
kiDNApped
Solar Island

**Other Works**
Blood Harbor: A Novel of Suspense
Lucifer's Machine (with Steven Savile)
Splashdown (with David Wood)
O.U.T.C.A.S.T. Ops series (with Rick Jones -
forthcoming)

**Writing as Jack Douglas**
Quake (With Douglas Corleone - forthcoming)

# PROLOGUE

*July 1543, off the coast of La Florida, New World*

**Juan Diego de** Guerrero emerged from his cabin onto the stern deck of the *Nuestra Señora de la San Pedro* and narrowed his eyes against the driving rain. It was not the precipitation that concerned him, however, but the wind that drove it and the sea's response to that steadily increasing force. He frowned, wiping cold salt spray from his weathered face as he gazed out on the marching waves, a single terrifying word dominating his mind: *Huracán.*

*I should have known.*

Upon waking with the sunrise he'd been pleased to see that they were beyond sight of land, well underway across the great Atlantic to his Spanish homeland. But even then he'd noticed the unusual conditions —the decreasing interval between swells, the electric tang in the air. Now these were undeniably magnified. It was like the hand of God pulling him back from his goal. Had he done something wrong?

"Captain, I was just coming to find you." Luis López de Olivares, Guerrero's first mate, skidded to a halt on the damp decking. His deeply tanned face was pale, and his calloused fingers worked with nervous energy. "The weather is turning against us."

He gave Guerrero a meaningful look, knowing he did not need to finish the thought.

Somewhat of a maverick, Guerrero had been warned about being caught in this part of the world during the summer months. But he had not planned things this way. It had taken him longer than he had anticipated to find what he was looking for and to load it into his ship's hold. Not satisfied with the usual bounty of gold, silver and jade figurines making their way to Europe in a steady stream from the New World, he had meandered much farther south than his contemporaries, in search of ever more exotic treasures and curiosities with which to impress King Charles. Eventually he had come to a southern land known to him only as *Río de la Plata*, where there were rumored to be entire river valleys lined with silver, complete mountain ranges made of the same.

"We will make it." Guerrero stilled his voice to a calm that he did not feel. "We always do."

Olivares turned to look out at the sea. "We shouldn't have traveled so far south. The silver wasn't worth it." The words came out in a low murmur, clearly not intended for Guerrero's ears, but the captain heard.

"It will be all right."

A pang of guilt caused Guerrero to wince. It wasn't prodigious amounts of silver that had drawn Guerrero months' worth of treacherous sailing out of his way. Early reports from his notable predecessors, including Amerigo Vespucci, had spawned provocative talk that Guerrero, then a child dockside laborer, had routinely eavesdropped on in the shadows of Spanish seaports. The explorers' gossip told of a wealth of strange and interesting minerals in addition to silver and gold, some of which had never before been witnessed in all of Europe. At the age of sixteen he would join the King's navy and for a time he forgot about the particulars of the tales of his youth, but still they drove his desire to remain at sea, to explore the world and locate its riches for Spain.

And so it was that decades later, after many false starts, tribulations and general hardships, he came to command the King's vessel, the treasure frigate *San Pedro*. It was also how he'd come to try the patience of his weary crew. Following an arduous coastal voyage, Guerrero's ship had landed at *Rio del Plata*. Guerrero himself spoke to the indigenous tribes who met them on the beach about the minerals he had heard of, and he was introduced in short order to a shaman who claimed that the stones had very special powers, perhaps to a dangerous degree.

The indigenous priest agreed to allow Guerrero's landing party to traverse their territory accompanied by local guides to a distant, rugged site where the natural resources might be excavated, but only under the condition that he first be allowed to bless the entire expedition in an elaborate ritual. To Guerrero, who reflected the widely held sentiment of Europe as a whole, these people were little more than savage heathens prone to the most base superstitions and animal urges, not yet having found the truth of Catholicism.

Olivares turned to face him, straightened his lanky

frame, and clenched his fists. "Captain. What *are* those stones?"

Only by sheer force of will did Guerrero maintain his calm. He wondered the same thing, though he was not about to admit it.

He had heard tales of these strange rocks for many years, though, and he thirsted for the chance to finally bring some back to Spain. At the same time, Guerrero knew that the time required for the overland trek would likely put him beyond his safe weather window for the return trip across the Atlantic, but he was on the voyage of a lifetime and it was a chance he was willing to take.

To Guerrero's men, however, the raw ore they painstakingly recovered and transported to the ship's cargo hold proved most unremarkable indeed. From whispered rumors of Guerrero's descriptions, the crew had been expecting some kind of lesser known gemstones—something that looked like rubies, garnets, maybe emeralds. But the rocks were plain-looking by comparison to those usually of value. Nothing they could easily trade in the ports of call for the favors of women and barkeeps. For these drab rocks they had trekked many miles through dank, insect-infested jungles and snake-filled swamps, scrabbled up and down the side of a bleak never-ending mountain of loose shale in order to extract examples of these rarest of New World specimens. A few of the men expressed dissatisfaction at going to such extremes to retrieve minerals not precisely known or valued rather than accepting more of the golden gifts readily offered by the coastal natives.

Guerrero had silenced the most vocal of these dissenters upon return to the ship by having them tied to the mast and whipped until dead while the rest of the crew was rewarded with a wine drenched feast. "Blood shall flow like wine for those who dare speak against his orders," he had shouted over the tortured cries of the condemned. For Guerrero, only absolute authority could command and control such a motley assortment of common men enduring long months at sea. His seafaring career had been long and varied, met overall with mixed success, and he was determined that this was the voyage with which he would finally make a lasting impression on the King.

But now, a sudden and vicious storm stood between him and that opportunity.

Guerrero ignored the question, took a deep breath, and looked down the decks of his hundred-foot-long ship. He was not surprised to see his crew already taking appropriate actions: reefing canvas, securing the cannons and various loose objects on deck, the helmsman adjusting course at the wheel to head them into the waves while barking orders to crew in the rigging.

"Was there something you needed from me, or did you think the middle of a storm was an appropriate time to debate my choice of cargo?"

Duly chastened, Olivares shook his head.

"In that case, resume your duties at once."

Olivares threw up a ragged salute, turned on his heel, and stalked away.

Guerrero clenched his fists. The mate was not

wrong. *I should have headed north sooner! Or perhaps if I had made the crossing to Africa and then headed north to Europe from there instead of travelling north into the heart of the New World...*

But as a wave crashed over the stern deck, the highest on the ship, and he watched a man fall to his death from the crow's nest, he knew that his second-guessing could no longer make a difference. It was a matter of mere hours at most before his ship would be ingested by a hurricane, and with God's blessing they would withstand the storm and be able to limp home. Without it, they would succumb to its fury.

With a last hurried glance at the wind-whipped whitecaps threatening his vessel, Guerrero retreated belowdecks and ran to the cargo hold. His feet sloshed through rank bilge water. He could have assigned crew to do this, but he wanted to personally supervise the securing of his most distinctive gifts. Reaching the wooden crates piled high with ore, he double-secured the ropes lashing the crates to the deck, then added more. He did not wish them to spill over and rip a hole in the hull. Satisfied, he was about to turn on a heel and head back topside when he paused.

Reaching into the nearest crate, he tossed chunks of ore aside until he found a flatter one and removed it. He used the tip of his machete to carve his initials into the rock, slicing a finger once when the rocking of the ship caused the blade to slip, and then thrust it into a pocket of his pantalones.

Were his dead body ever to be brought back to Spain, he desired proof that Juan Diego de Guerrero, the boy who had labored for his entire childhood as a petty dockworker fetching items for sailors, had now retrieved something that would one day light the world on fire.

*July 21, 1961, 300 miles off Cape Canaveral, Florida*

**NASA space capsule** *Liberty Bell 7* dangled from its drogue parachute at an altitude of 1,200 feet. Returning from a successful suborbital flight in a demonstration of emerging United States space power, it was now about to land back on Earth as planned, by splashing down into in the Atlantic Ocean. A small flotilla of support ships and helicopters waited below to retrieve the capsule as soon as it hit the water. Inside the spacecraft, Gus Grissom, among the first wave of a new breed of fliers known as "astronauts," spoke into his radio, his gravelly voice exuding a calm professionalism.

"Atlantic ship Capcom, this is *Liberty Bell 7*, do you read me, over?"

The reply was near instant. "Bell 7, this is Atlantic ship Capcom. I read you loud and clear, over."

"Roger that, Capcom. My rate of descent is twenty-nine feet per second, fuel has been dumped for impact, over."

"Copy that, Bell 7. We are tracking your descent. Everything looks A-okay, over."

For the next few seconds, all eyes on the support ships and aircraft were focused on the falling space capsule. Then the radio channel crackled again.

"Capcom reporting: Splashdown! We have splashdown! Bell 7, a helicopter will reach you in about thirty seconds, over."

The space capsule, shaped roughly like the American iconic symbol for which it was named, complete with a "crack" painted down its side, was about as seaworthy as a cork. It bobbed helplessly in the water, capable of nothing more than drifting until it could be picked up by a helicopter. A tense couple of seconds passed while those listening to the radio frequency waited to see if the astronaut inside the capsule had been knocked around too badly upon hitting the water to reply.

But then Grissom said, "Roger that, 'chute has been jettisoned. I'll be going over my post-flight checklist. As soon as that's done I'll be ready for evac, over."

Broadcast radio commentators intended for audiences listening around the world remarked how thorough and professional Gus Grissom was, that he would rather complete his checklists before leaving the capsule for the comforts of the helicopter and ships even after all he'd endured. The big Huey hovered overhead until they heard Grissom's voice over the communications line once again.

"*Liberty Bell 7* to Capcom. Now prepared for evac, over."

The Huey moved into position over the floating capsule. A cable was lowered from the helicopter.

Suddenly the hatch cover of the spacecraft was seen popping off the craft.

Fitted with explosive bolts for emergency evacuation from the inside, under normal circumstances it was meant to be opened not by the astronaut but by rescue personnel once the capsule had been secured back aboard its transport ship. That ship was aircraft carrier *USS Randolph*, and from its bridge a mission recovery team coordinator frowned beneath a pair of binoculars.

"Grissom's out of the capsule, he's in the water!" he told the radioman, who promptly relayed that message to the pilot of the helicopter, who was told in no uncertain terms to pursue the capsule. Grissom's spacesuit was designed to provide him with flotation, but they had no way of knowing now whether it really worked. What they did know was that without the hatch cover in place, America's space race investment was rapidly flooding with water and would soon be lost to the depths if not secured.

A helicopter crewman descended from the aircraft and connected a cable to the spacecraft. While Grissom floated nearby, buffeted by rotor wash that whipped up the sea surface into a frothy foam, the rescue crew member was winched back into the chopper. The Huey's pilot then managed to lift the capsule a few feet out of the water, but could gain no further altitude, the entire rig slanting dangerously toward the sea.

"Capsule's full of water, we can't lift it!" came the frantic radio transmission to mission support personnel. One more attempt at airlifting the swamped spaceship was made, but to no avail. The laws of physics, to whose mastery the entire mission owed its success to this point, could not be broken. The helicopter could simply not provide enough lift, and the rescue craft itself started to wobble precariously scant feet above the waves.

"Cut the cable, cut the cable!" came the command from Capcom, but the quickness with which the task was carried out made it likely that the helicopter crew hadn't been waiting for orders.

The cable was severed. The capsule dropped back into the sea.

The chopper's pilot, now free of his weighty burden, quickly regained control of the aircraft and maneuvered to pick up the floating astronaut.

Gus Grissom was hauled aboard without further incident, while below them all, *Liberty Bell 7* continued its mission alone to the distant seafloor.

# CHAPTER 1

*April 2, 1999, Monterey, California*

**U.S. Navy SEAL** Dane Maddock tightened his grip on the submersible's control joystick as he eased the *Deep Surveyor III* into a narrow crevice nearly a mile beneath the Pacific. His co-pilot in the two-person craft, fellow SEAL Uriah "Bones" Bonebrake, pointed off to their right where the rock wall of the submarine canyon they'd been following slid past them mere feet away.

"Easy bro, maybe two feet clearance on this side," Bones warned.

"That's more room than I usually have to park at those sleazy clubs you drag me to."

Surprisingly to Dane, Bones remained silent. The six-and-a-half foot tall Cherokee rarely worried about anything, a testament to the fact that he did not consider being a mile underwater in a plastic bubble to be the time or place for levity. Dane cast a sideways glance to Bones' side of their acrylic sphere, where he kept a sharp eye on the irregular canyon wall.

This outing was to be their checkout dive for an intensive program that capped four straight weeks of submersible pilot training. Completing the dive's objective would earn them a new qualification, and Bones in particular was not looking forward to failing.

"Just stay focused, man. This isn't really a course I want to repeat."

Dane looked over at his co-pilot. "You mean you don't think this is fun?"

"Never been this deep in one of these things. Plus, I have to trust your driving." He let out a loud sigh. "I'm sure I'll get used to it sooner or later."

"You wound me. I thought we were like two peas in a pod in here!"

"I'd sell all my naked photos of your mom if it would buy me the amount of room a pea must have compared to this. And you've got quite a bit more legroom than me."

Just shy of six feet, Dane did in fact have more space to maneuver within the racks of electronic equipment that guided the craft and allowed it to do useful work. For Bones, on the other hand, although he was, like all SEALs, a superb swimmer, scuba diver and all-around naval warrior, being cramped in the close confines of an underwater vehicle for hours at a time was losing its luster.

Still, he was here for a reason, and that reason was that while Dane had qualified as an ace submersible pilot, Bones had excelled at manipulating the sub's grab-arms and other specialized payload equipment in the simulation testing and training sessions with remotely operated vehicles, or ROVs. Dane had been taken aback when he read the duty assignment roster and saw Bones' name beside his own. The big Indian was always surprising him. Somehow he just kept showing up, which meant that somebody with a higher pay grade than Dane's saw something in the guy. Bones had a certain directness about him, a no-nonsense approach to everyday life situations that sometimes rankled the more reserved Dane, but by now the two had worked together enough that their professionalism had begun to overcome the irritations that initially flared up between them. Most of the time.

"Hey, where you going, Maddock? Our target's down there." Bones pointed down between his feet into the abyss that seemed to stretch below them into Hell itself. Their sonar told them, though, that the canyon's bottom lay "only" another mile deeper. Fortunately to both of them, they were not required to go that far.

"You sure?" Dane manipulated the ship's controls so that they were poised between two rock walls, awaiting confirmation. Bathed in the harsh artificial light of the sub's halogen floodlights, the walls revealed their true colors in a world normally immersed in total blackness. Strange blue sponges that resembled lichens, vertical fields of white anemones, and myriad other creatures Dane couldn't identify somehow eked out a living down here in this freezing world of immense pressure. But as unique as it was, most of it looked the same to him.

Bones interrupted his thoughts. "In the briefing I was actually awake for, they said the target was 'at lower depth than where the canyon wall convergence narrows to less than three meters.' I did some checking and found that the target usually lives on a flat area. So we go down from here and look for a rocky shelf, I guess."

In response, Dane shot Bones a grudging look of respect and tilted their craft downward, activating the forward thrusters. For all his boisterousness, Bones somehow also found a way to pay attention, no matter how much he pretended otherwise. And theirs was definitely a line of work where not paying attention could get you killed.

They dropped down through the narrow crevice, Dane tweaking the sub's controls to make sure they didn't scrape the walls while Bones directed a movable spotlight to their surroundings while also monitoring their depth and sonar readouts.

"Coming up on something," Dane said, easing back on the thrusters.

"Rocky shelf. This could be it. Look for the… There it is!" Bones adjusted the angle of his high intensity beam until it illuminated a whitish stalk towering perhaps ten feet, its red tip a few feet below their submersible's belly. "Take us down a few feet; then we curve with the wall to the right."

Dane executed the delicate maneuver until they hovered over a flat expanse of rock that reminded him of a stairway landing—a brief interruption of the vertical plunge the canyon took for yet another mile. There, in the center of the platform, grew a massive tubeworm. Pale crabs scuttled out of reach of the craft's floodlights, pouring off the rocky shelf into the water column beneath them like lemmings from a cliff.

"Are we sure this is the right tubeworm?" Dane's careful attention to the controls didn't allow him the luxury of taking in the details of their surroundings to the degree that Bones could.

"Surer than you were about that dude in a dress who hit on you last weekend. I'm looking at the marker right next to it."

Dane took his co-pilot's word that the small cement block that had been previously placed there by their sub instructors lay at the foot of the towering invertebrate.

"Roger that. The marker; not the guy in the dress. And, for the record, it was a girl, she was just…"

"A big, hairy dude?"

Ignoring Bones' jibe, Dane brought their submersible closer to the base of the creature, which swayed slightly with the vehicle's prop-wash.

Bones leaned forward, pressing his head against the sub's acrylic dome as he stared intently at their target. "Okay, stop. I'm within range of the manipulator arm."

Dane let up on the thrusters. "Do your thing."

Clutched in the metal claw at the end of an extensible arm outside the sub was a tubular metal object. Bones delicately pressed buttons that rotated the claw as well as the arm itself in different directions. "I wish we were placing some C4 explosives instead of this boring contraption," he said, referring to the scientific instrumentation package they were supposed to deploy. "That would be much more awesome." He deftly placed the device on the ledge next to the cement marker and released it from the sub's grab arm.

"That's why this is *practice*, Bones. We screw up with this thing and some eggheads don't find out what the temperature variations are down here when that worm farts. Make a mistake with C4 and maybe these canyon walls come…"

A gruff, all-business voice issuing from their communications channel interrupted him. *"Topside to Deep Surveyor III, you are ordered to report immediately to Base Command. Proceed to support ship at once, do you copy?"*

Dane looked over at Bones, who was still retracting the now empty manipulator arm back to the sub. When Bones completed that task he looked over at Dane, raising his eyebrows.

Dane said to Bones, "What'd you do, drop the science package over the cliff?"

Bones shook his head and pointed down at the metal cylinder, where a green LED glowed next to the worm. "It's all good."

Dane responded over the radio that he acknowledged the order, then put his hands to work on the sub's controls.

"Let's go find out what they want."

**An hour later** Dane and Bones strode into the lobby of SEAL Base Command, Monterey Station. Dane addressed a female receptionist in uniform seated behind a horseshoe shaped desk. He started to explain who they were when she waved him down.

"In here now, gentlemen!" a male voice pre-empted from the office, the door to which was open but the man out of sight. The young woman raised an eyebrow and tilted her head in the direction of the office, her meaning clear. *You'd better go.*

Bones gave her his most lascivious smile which she returned before swiveling in her chair to answer a phone call. Dane reached the doorway to Senior Commander Douglas Lawhorne's private office first, where he gave a salute.

"Close the door behind you, and at ease."

As soon as Bones stepped inside, Dane shut the door and then the two of them took seats in front of the commander's desk, which was set off to the left of the well-appointed room. Scale model ships and submarines decorated the walls behind the desk, while the fourth floor floor-to-ceiling windows afforded a magnificent view of Monterey Bay and the waters from which they had just returned. But it wasn't often a newly minted SEAL was summoned directly to a commander's office in the middle of a training exercise, so for the moment Dane refrained from absorbing the atmosphere. He noticed that even Bones, whom he considered a good ADHD candidate, was so far affording the commander his undivided attention.

"Congratulations on earning your Deep Manned Submersible Rating, you two. Well done." Lawhorne's smile did not reach his eyes.

Dane and Bones exchanged quizzical looks that said, *we passed?* But then the commander, a balding man in his early fifties with a chest full of medals, spoke again.

"Your instructor tells me that you both scored highly throughout the exercises. I'm sorry that I don't yet have your detailed evaluations ready for review, or your new pins, but you'll receive them as soon as you get back."

Dane let the obvious question go unspoken, as he felt it was not his place to question a man of the commander's rank unprompted.

"Get back from where?" Bones asked.

Dane did his best to suppress an involuntary cringe. He looked over at his partner in war, who sat casually in his jeans and wool pullover—the same outfit he'd had on in the sub to ward off the chill. A small abalone shell hung around his neck, a nod to the native tribes who once lived in California for whom the shiny-shelled mollusk was an important food source. Dane expected Lawhorne might rebuke Bones for speaking out of turn, but if the officer was irritated he didn't let it show.

"The two of you have been placed on special assignment to the east coast of Florida, effective immediately. That's all I know at this point."

Lawhorne paused to look at his two SEALs as if he expected questions, so Dane ventured, "Pardon me, Sir, but are you going to brief us?"

The man on the other side of the desk shook his head emphatically. "Negative. I am not privy to the details of your assignment because I do not have sufficient clearance."

Dane's mouth started to drop open before he pulled it together. Bones also said nothing, an indicator that he too was stunned by the implications of their superior officer's words.

If *he* didn't have clearance, then how high-level must this assignment be?

The commander checked his watch. "You board a plane in fifty-three minutes. I'm told you'll be briefed en route. Get back to your quarters. Pack your bags, wait for ground transport. Dismissed."

Dane shot to his feet and saluted. Bones ambled up from his chair, saluting with a confused look on his face. Then he said, "Excuse me, Sir, but does this mean we're going to miss the submersible class graduation party that was supposed to be tonight, or will it be rescheduled?"

Dane rolled his eyes and rubbed his temples.

"Son, you're going to miss that party but from the way it seems, if you have success on this mission I expect you'll be coming home to the biggest damn bash you've ever had in your life."

Lawhorne saw the grin forming on Bones' face and held up a hand before continuing. "Listen to me. Like I said, I don't have the details. But this much I do know: your country needs you. Do *not* let it down."

# CHAPTER 2

**Dane cracked a** smile as he watched Bones duck under the doorway to the Learjet 35. The private plane was by far the nicest mode of transportation they'd taken thus far in their military careers, though certainly not the largest. Accommodating six passengers plus a crew of three, it made up in style what it lacked in size. An attractive flight attendant with strawberry blonde hair and a sprinkling of freckles across her button nose led Dane and Bones away from the cockpit, the mahogany door to which was closed, to two leather recliners, one each on opposite sides of a plush carpeted aisle. Behind these two seats, a drawn curtain divided the cabin; murmurs of soft conversation drifted in from the other side.

Dane sank into his chair while Bones stood there in the aisle, mouth agape, taking in the splendor. "One time I flew first class commercial because I got bumped from standby, but this makes that look like a cattle car," he said, slipping into his seat like a man sitting down in his Lazy Boy to watch TV after dinner, a leg flopped over one of the chair arms. "This rocks. I never fit an airline seat."

"Please sit upright and buckle up for takeoff, sir. As soon as we're at cruising altitude you're free to do what you wish." The flight attendant's sharp tone belied her farm girl looks.

Bones turn his attention to the flight attendant, his gaze lingering over her crisply pressed uniform, and grinned. Dane tensed, wondering what might come out of the big Indian's mouth next, but Bones complied, giving the young woman a wink as he clicked his seatbelt closed.

"Sure beats the heck out of trying to sleep in the cargo net of a C-130 transport next to everybody's crap bouncing around, right?" Dane asked.

"Bro, you got that right! Remember that time on the way out to Honolulu…"

Bones was in the middle of recounting an anecdote about a loose surfboard waking him up in the cargo hold when the Lear pilot's voice came over the intercom letting them know that they would be flying non-stop from Monterey to Cape Canaveral.

"I'll be back in a few minutes to see if you gentlemen would like anything to eat or drink," the flight attendant told them before retreating to the front of the plane.

Dane and Bones settled back and allowed the takeoff forces to pin them to their cushy seats. In short order they said goodbye to the Pacific, where the sun was already sinking lower in the sky as the aircraft banked into a turn toward the east.

True to her word, when the aircraft leveled off, the flight attendant returned with menus. Both men ordered three-course meals of spicy Mexican food along with bottles of Dos Equis. It had been a long day in the submersible and their sudden orders had left them with no time to eat until now. They feasted, saying little while they enjoyed the tang of cilantro and marinated beef, lost in thought about what might lay ahead.

No sooner had they cleared their plates than they heard the curtain behind them slide open.

"If you two gentlemen would be so kind as to join us in the conference room for your briefing, we'll tell you what you're doing aboard this flying luxury suite. This way please."

Dane and Bones sat up and turned around. A naval officer they had never seen before stood behind them. Dane hastily wiped his mouth with a napkin before standing straight and saluting. Bones did the same and the officer briefly returned their salutes. The pair of SEALs followed him into the middle section of the jet, which had been sectioned off into a nicely appointed yet highly functional work area. A hardwood conference table occupied the center of the space, with leather office chairs fixed in place around it. A large LCD monitor was mounted on one wall. Paper nautical charts were spread out on the table itself, along with a bevy of open laptops. In addition to the officer who had escorted them back here, Dane and Bones were greeted by three other men, all of whom appeared to be in their late fifties. Two of them wore military uniforms while a third was dressed in a suit and tie.

Dane was stunned to recognize the insignia of a Navy admiral on one of their lapels. He did not recognize the other uniform and was correct in his assumption that it was not Navy. The admiral nodded to the naval officer, who promptly stepped around Dane and Bones to draw the curtain across the cabin.

"Gentlemen, please be seated," the Admiral began. Dane and Bones followed the order, sitting next to one another in the only two available chairs. The admiral continued.

"I am Admiral Jeffrey Whitburn, based at the Pentagon, where I'll be returning after we let you two off at Canaveral. Let me begin by saying that both of you come very highly recommended and it's a pleasure to have you here."

"Thanks. We think you're pretty cool too!" Bones blurted. Dane kicked him in the shin under the table.

The admiral seemed unsurprised by the comment. If he'd done his homework, he probably knew at least a little bit about Bones' eccentricities.

"By way of introductions, the gentleman who brought you back here is Captain James Epson. Seated across from me is U.S. Air Force General Marcus Holloway, who sits on the Joint Chiefs of Staff."

Dane felt a strange numbness come over him as the sheer magnitude of whatever assignment they were about to be asked to do hit home. Joint Chiefs of Staff? He shot a quick glance over at Bones, whose puzzled expression clearly said, *What the…?*

"Gentlemen: I'll get right to the point. We'll tell you what you need to know, nothing more. Don't ask questions. We're telling you everything we can. A lot of very smart people, smarter than us, have developed the plan of action we're about to brief you on."

Bones raised his hand like a kid in a classroom. The admiral scowled at him but waited for him to speak. Bones said, "Sir, are these smart people in the military?"

"Bonebrake, you do realize you just asked a question after I said not to? I can answer this one, but don't let it happen again, is that clear?"

"Yes, sir, it's clear."

Dane couldn't help but notice that Bones had not apologized. The guy was ballsy.

"Most of those who developed this mission are not in the military per se, but work for U.S. intelligence agencies that advise the military branches, including Mr. Sardowski, here, who is an analyst with the CIA based out of Langley."

The guy in the suit gave Dane and Bones a curt nod. Dane and Bones sat still and mute as they processed this revelation. *Central Intelligence Agency?*

The admiral continued while the naval officer presented Dane and Bones with a paper form and a pen.

"We know that as SEALs you're sworn to secrecy on every mission. But before we begin let me stress that this goes far beyond that. In order to participate in this assignment, you'll need to be given Top Secret clearance. We've already taken the necessary steps to expedite the process. All you need to do is to sign the papers in front of you. But a word of caution. Not a single syllable of what you're about to hear in this airplane ever comes out of your lips, is that understood? No matter how drunk you get at a party," he said, staring at Bones for emphasis, who nodded his agreement while signing the document. Dane took a bit more time to read his, but also signed. While the officer snatched away the papers, the admiral resumed his talk.

"Our goal is to deliver your briefing with time left over for you to get as much sleep as possible. You're about to embark on one hell of an assignment. So listen up, here we go."

He nodded to Captain Epson, who promptly pressed a key on a remote control, activating a PowerPoint presentation on the wall-mounted screen. A photo of what looked to Dane and Bones like some kind of early diving bell sitting on a wheeled platform appeared on the screen.

Epson directed a laser pointer in a circular motion around the object on the monitor.

"This is NASA space capsule *Liberty Bell 7*." He let that sink in for a moment on the bemused Dane and Bones as he advanced to the next slide. It also depicted the capsule on a wheeled platform, but in this shot a spacesuited astronaut stood next to the craft.

Epson went on. "This photo was taken in 1961, shortly before the capsule splashed down in the Atlantic Ocean, three hundred miles off Cape Canaveral, not far from the Bahamas, and was lost in a retrieval accident. Gus Grissom, the lone occupier of the capsule, was rescued, while the capsule sank to the seafloor. It has remained there for the last thirty-eight years undisturbed, at a depth of almost three miles, or 15,000 feet."

The admiral's gaze shifted to the marine chart laid out on the table, and Dane and Bones followed suit. "We believe it to be a flat, featureless bottom," he noted, dragging a pointer finger across the chart. Then he looked up at the Air Force General, who stared right at Dane and Bones while he spoke.

"The Mercury-Redstone 4 mission, so-named for the rocket that carried the Liberty Bell crew capsule as part of the Mercury manned space program that preceded the more famous Apollo series, had two agendas." The General looked around the table at his colleagues as if to see if any of them would object to where he was going. None of them indicated as such, so the Joint Chiefs of Staff representative resumed his delivery to a mystified Dane and Bones.

"The official, publicly known agenda was a short suborbital flight to demonstrate America's space prowess to the Russians. You boys weren't even born yet, but at the time the Cold War was heating up with Russia having launched their Sputnik satellite a few years earlier, and from there the space race was on."

Dane nodded. He'd always been fascinated by the space race and the Apollo moon missions in particular.

"But the unofficial agenda of that mission is why you're here today. As I said, the U.S. was looking to use the fourth Mercury mission as a message to the world, and in particular the Soviets, that America was the preeminent space power. But beyond that, the Kennedy Administration had something up their sleeve."

Dane looked away from the photo of Grissom and the capsule on screen to gauge the faces of the other men. All of them appeared dead-serious, almost grimly determined. Dane saw the Admiral eye the General and lift a hand in his direction from where it had been resting on the table. *Stop.*

The Admiral took over. "*Liberty Bell 7* carried a as

part of her payload a small nuclear bomb."

Dane gave a low whistle. For a few seconds the only sound was the rumble of the jet's engines as they cut through the evening sky.

The Admiral spoke up again. "We can't tell you why that device was on board, so don't ask."

The General nodded and then resumed his talk by clicking to the next slide.

"This shot was taken from a U.S. Navy air craft carrier, and shows Gus Grissom treading water while the Liberty capsule is flooding. Poor ol' Gus was blamed for the rest of his career and even afterwards for accidentally blowing the explosive hatch bolts prematurely."

Dane could almost hear Bones' gears churning to put out a dirty joke, but the loquacious Indian seemed to realize he'd pushed right up to the edge with his earlier question, and he remained silent along with the rest of the room.

"But the truth is, he did it on purpose. He did it to sink that capsule because of what it contained on board: an unexploded nuclear bomb that no one was supposed to know about," the General interjected once again, reading the questions apparent on the SEALs' faces. "The reason the bomb was never detonated, and that no one has ever heard of a nuclear weapon aboard a U.S. spacecraft, was because of Gus Grissom. Once he was in space, apparently he got cold feet and refused to carry out his orders. He got scared or something. The psychologists still aren't exactly sure—but the upshot of it was that he absolutely would not cooperate to carry out the flight objective, making the working atmosphere non-conducive to completing the mission."

"So instead," the Admiral resumed, "it was arranged that NASA would announce they had successfully completed a short sub-orbital hop that just happened to have a little glitch on splashdown. They carried a few ordinary science experiments aboard, nothing special."

Sardowski made his voice heard for the first time since the briefing began. "The end result of all this is that the A-bomb is still resting inside the capsule on the ocean floor," he stated. "And until now that hasn't posed much of a problem. Back in 1961, deliberately sinking that capsule was a good move if you didn't want it to be found. Undersea salvage capabilities were far behind what's needed to raise the capsule. But in recent years that began to change, and very recently..." The CIA man paused to hit a key on his laptop, advancing the slide to one that showed the logo of a popular cable television network.

"...the TV network, The *Science Channel* mounted a privately funded expedition to locate the spacecraft on the ocean floor. Interestingly enough, for a while it looked like they would be unsuccessful, although they did find a wreck of another sort— one that historians agree is most likely a sixteenth-century Spanish treasure ship."

"And that find has a lot of unwanted attention converging on the area," the General chimed in.

"Yes," the Admiral said, "but since then the TV expedition succeeded in locating the capsule and have made a series of preliminary unmanned dives to it with a remotely operated vehicle. CIA intelligence shows that they are now on site preparing to make a serious attempt at raising *Liberty Bell 7*. They, of course, have no idea that a nuclear bomb rests inside that capsule."

The analyst clicked off the overhead monitor, casting the room a shade darker. The admiral spoke next, leveling a steely gaze at Dane and Bones.

"And we have direct orders from the President of the United States to make certain it stays that way. We need you two to ensure that the network's effort to raise the capsule is not successful. We need you to do this as quietly as possible. The optimal outcome would be for you to extract the nuclear payload from the capsule before anyone knows about it and bring it to us. Failing that, either destroy the bomb on the seafloor—without getting yourselves killed. Or, as a last resort…"

The admiral trailed off, eyeing the CIA agent, who finished his sentence for him.

"…make sure that the television expedition meets with an accident."

# CHAPTER 3

*Atlantic Ocean, 288 miles off Cape Canaveral*

**The fishing trawler** *F/V Atlantic Pride* wasn't much to look at. Steaming east at a leisurely cruising speed, the streaks of rust on her hull and the plume of black exhaust from her chugging diesel told a casual observer that this was a tired, aging workhorse of a boat, perhaps a couple of seasons away from the end of her useful life. This image was carefully chosen, however, in order to provide a rustic veneer over what was in fact a state-of-the-art special warfare platform for the U.S. Navy.

Dane stood at the helm of the nondescript vessel while beside him in the wheelhouse Bones monitored the radar, sonar and chartplotters. Upon landing in Cape Canaveral, they'd been driven to Port Canaveral where they boarded the *Atlantic Pride* in the wee hours of the morning. They were then given a full tour of its layout, functionality and covert features by Captain Epson, who wished them "Godspeed" and left Dane and Bones on the vessel. The SEAL duo had the boat underway shortly after that, still under cover of darkness.

Now early afternoon, they'd motored all day to reach this remote area of the Atlantic. After initially inspecting the boat's engine compartment, Dane had expressed concern to Epson that it would take far too long to get three hundred miles offshore, but Epson had smiled and bent down to a concealed hatch cover overlain with a carefully placed application of grime. Lifting the cover, Epson had beamed while he pointed out a gleaming set of twin Volvo diesels. "Less than fifty hours on these things," he'd said, explaining, "To get you out there fast, there's a concealed switch on the instrument panel, underneath the weather fax. Flip that and you shut off the original engine and switch to the new twins. Just remember to switch back to the old when you approach the site, because you want to look like an old, slow fishing trawler, not something that can do forty knots all day long."

Both had appreciated the features of the old scow, including the redundancy of the three engines, as well as the other special features Epson had pointed out.

Now, approaching the capsule salvage area, Bones lifted a pair of marine binoculars and scanned the waters ahead. He had reached the end of his arc when the glint of sunlight off metal arrested his gaze. "Got something." He steadied himself with one arm on the instrument console.

"There she is! *R/V Ocean Explorer*," Bones said, giving the name they were told in the latter portion of their briefing was that of the *Science Channel*'s research vessel. "Pretty big boat. A ship, I'd call it."

"Let me have a look." Bones handed Dane the binoculars and he scoped out the television expedition's vessel. "Yeah, geez. Got to be almost a hundred and fifty feet. Converted mega-yacht, looks like. They don't look like they're under power right now."

Dane handed the glasses back to Bones and flipped the switch that would activate the old engine. The deceptive trawler slowed, but kept heading toward the salvage site.

"Hey Maddock," Bones said from underneath the binoculars. "I see some activity on the stern deck. Looks like a camera crew."

Dane gave a quick laugh. "Out of all the targets a SEAL could be asked to engage with, I'll take a camera crew aboard a modified luxury yacht any day."

"I hear you," Bones said, setting aside the binoculars and turning to his associate. "It seems a hell of a lot easier than extracting some diplomat from a Liberian oil tanker off the coast of Somalia, you remember that?"

"Don't remind me."

"I know. But at the same time…" Bones trailed off.

"At the same time what?" Dane wanted Bones to clear whatever it was that seemed to be weighing on him off his chest before they got any closer to the site.

"I don't know if I…" Bones stalled again.

"You don't know if you could kill civilians to protect the secrets of our mission?"

"Yeah. I mean, those are our orders, right? 'Make sure they have an accident.' That sucks."

"That's a last resort," Dane reminded him. "We'll do everything we can to make sure it doesn't come to that."

"But if it *does* come to that…"

A flash of light on the water caught their attention.

"Hold on, did you see that?" Dane asked.

"White flash?"

"Yeah. Gotta be a good nautical mile from the TV ship, too."

Bones saw a second blip light up on their radar circle and grabbed for the binoculars. "It's another boat, just flipping on their deck lights for the evening, looks like."

"Part of the TV expedition?"

Bones examined the ship again. After a while he said, "It looks like they're towing something. Let's move in for a closer look."

Dane glanced over at the *Ocean Explorer*, then back to the mystery ship before throttling up and heading toward the latter. He looked down on the work deck once and then back to Bones, as if thinking about something.

"Before we get too close we should get out on deck and do some fishing. It's part of our cover," he said. He opened a storage locker and grabbed a couple of rod-and-reel combos. "We can just fish and watch them from the deck, try to see what they're up to."

Bones indicated his agreement and Dane set the boat to a trolling speed, engaging the auto-pilot so that it would hold its course and then the two of them went out to the work deck.

"I've done a lot of trout fishing in North Carolina, but not much ocean fishing," Bones said. "You know what you're doing?"

Dane looked up from the lure he was tying onto his line. "I lived most of my life in Florida. I know my way around a deep sea fishing rig. Way out here we'll probably catch something pretty quick."

"Won't it look funny for a commercial boat to be using rod and reels, though?"

"No, just heading from one spot to the next the commercial guys sometimes fish for fun. I think it's best to have some kind of activity on deck when we first approach. I can almost feel the binoculars on us now." Dane and Bones gazed at the two ships in the distance.

"Let's give it a try." Dane set up Bones' rig and then the two of them cast their lines into the boat's wake. While they waited for a strike, Bones monitored the mystery ship, focusing with his binoculars on its tow rig.

"What do you think? Magnetometer?" he asked, referring to a kind of high-tech metal detector used in deep water shipwreck searches. He passed the binoculars to Dane, who directed them at the ship.

"Definitely a magnetometer. They're coming back around now, too, to start another leg of their grid pattern. They're searching for something made of metal down there. The Spanish ship itself was made of wood, of course, but its treasure, if it carried gold and silver, would register."

"If the show made it known where they found the treasure wreck, why do they have to search for it?"

"It's not unusual for portions of a wreck to be scattered over a large area, even miles. Especially one that sank in water this deep, probably in a storm. You can picture it breaking into pieces on the way down and then those pieces settle on the seafloor in a long debris trail."

"So the *Science Channel* people could have found only part of the wreck, and now these guys are looking around to see what else they might have missed?"

"That'd be my guess." Dane handed the binoculars to Bones.

"But why wouldn't the *Science Channel* also be interested in the Spanish wreck, keeping that discovery to themselves? Why announce it?"

"Probably because the TV expedition is not really focused on the shipwreck. They want the capsule. They may even be renting equipment that they only have a set number of days to use, and it's going to take all their concentration and resources to be able to pull that spacecraft salvage off. After all, if they're successful, it'd be the deepest commercial salvage operation ever done. So they decided to stir the publicity pot a little by announcing the treasure ship. It could…"

Suddenly the fishing rods—first Dane's and then Bones'—bent sharply at the tips and they heard a rapid clicking noise as line spooled from the reels.

"Fish on!" Dane said, yanking his rod out of the holder. He let the fish run until it soared from the water, glistening in the light.

"What is it?" Bones picked up his rod and almost lost it over the side before he realized how much strength he needed.

"Yellowfin tuna!" Dane said. "We'll be eating good tonight." He briefly coached Bones on how to fight the gamefish and then went back to reeling in his own.

Bracing the butt of the pole against his midsection, Dane pulled up on it, feeling his biceps burn with the effort. Pull up, reel down, repeat. It was a familiar set of actions to him, and for a little while he almost forgot that he was a highly trained naval operative on a dangerous undercover assignment. The faint smell of diesel in his nostrils, the salt spray flicking from the spooling line peppering his face... it took him back to the days of his youth, fishing Florida waters. He squinted his eyes against the sun-dappled ocean where the majestic fish thrashed and pulled for its life.

Soon the sound of splashing yanked Dane out of his reverie and he was staring at a fish whipping the water behind the boat into a frenzy. He reached over the side with a gaff and hooked his tuna behind a gill, hauling it aboard where it slapped hard against the deck.

Bones almost had his tuna to the boat by sheer brute force, and Dane told him to pull up on it while he readied the gaff again. In one smooth motion he hooked the second fish and tossed it over the rail.

"Not bad, right?" Dane said to Bones, who was grinning ear to ear while looking at the pair of tuna on deck. In addition to the cover, Dane had also hoped that the fishing would help him bond with his partner. They got along well enough most of the time after a rocky start in BUDS school, but the relationship was still being forged and for this mission above all others, they would need to respect one another. Dane knew that the wily Cherokee felt he was too by-the-book at times, too safe.

He removed the titanium dive knife he wore clipped to his belt and proceeded to filet his fish on the deck, throwing the scraps over the side.

"You're as good at that as I am at skinning a deer," Bones noted.

"Spent every summer fishing while I was growing up. At least, the years we lived in Florida. Caught tons of yellowfins just like these."

"This is my first one," Bones said with a hint of pride.

"No way! Well then you've got to do the ritual."

Bones gave him a skeptical look.

"Seriously." Dane bent to the big fish with his knife and made a few deep cuts. After a minute he withdrew his bloodied hand from the animal and held out a small globule of dark red meat for Bones' inspection. It quivered slightly in his palm.

"The heart."

Dane popped the morsel into his mouth and swallowed, enjoying the look of surprise on Bone's face as he chased it with a swig from a bottle of water. "The ultimate sushi," he said, wiping his mouth. "It's good luck to eat the heart from your first tuna. Try it with yours."

Dane knew he was appealing to Bones' native American instincts. In short order he had extracted the powerful muscle from the tuna Bones had boated. The hefty Indian took the piece of meat and held it up for closer inspection. "When I killed my first deer, my uncle spread its blood over my face. I guess this is the fish version." He glanced over the boat's rail toward the ships they were monitoring. "I guess I could use all the luck I can get, too." He tipped his head back and dropped the heart into his mouth. Like Dane, he swallowed it whole and chased it with water.

"How is it?"

"Tastes like chicken." Bones grinned.

The two SEALs looked one another in the eye. They were in this together now, in a way that went beyond the non-disclosure agreements they'd signed aboard the Learjet.

Then they heard the radio, rigged such that it was broadcast over a loudspeaker system to be heard when not in the wheelhouse, crackle to life.

*"Calling fishing trawler, this is research vessel* Ocean Explorer, *please reply!"*

# CHAPTER 4

**Dane and Bones** ran to the trawler's pilothouse where Dane picked up the radio and keyed the transmitter.

"Attention *R/V Ocean Explorer*, this is fishing trawler *Atlantic Pride* acknowledging your transmission." Dane repeated his message one more time before they received a reply.

"Atlantic Pride, *you are advised to fish away from this area, which is now the site of a deep water salvage operation. Fishing gear in the water may interfere with salvage operations. Do you copy?*"

Bones glanced through his binoculars at the salvage ship in the distance. "They worried we might snag their ROV cables with our lines from a mile away?"

Dane held the transmitter at the ready without keying it while he weighed the question. "More than likely they just don't want anyone around. But let's have a little fun." He spoke into the microphone.

"We copy. We'll stay clear." He kept his tone casual. "Mind if we ask what you're salvaging?"

Bones raised his eyebrows. Would they be truthful? But the reply was easygoing.

"*Space capsule on the bottom. We're filming for a Science Channel cable special.*"

Dane grinned at Bones as he replied. "Cool! I wouldn't mind getting a look at that. When do you plan to bring it up?"

Bones' eyes bugged out at the directness of the questions. But once again, the television crew's representative seemed unfazed by the line of inquiry. Why shouldn't they be open when they had no reason to believe anyone would want the capsule more than they did?

*"We're in the middle of some last minute prep work now, but weather permitting we're looking at starting the actual salvage tomorrow morning. I'd advise you give us a wide berth. Never know what might go wrong."*

Dane and Bones exchanged a concerned glance, and Dane said off air, "I was hoping we'd have a day or two to get a feel for the situation, but if they're going to try and raise the *Liberty Bell* tomorrow then we've got to do something tonight."

Bones gave a heavy sigh. The people backing their orders had acted just in time. He nodded.

Dane resumed his radio exchange. "Good luck and thanks for the heads up. We'll stay out of your way. Oh, one more question if you have a second?"

Bones gave a silent laugh. Dane was really pushing the intel gathering, but they were short on time, so why not?

*"Go ahead."*

"Is that other ship about a mile to your southeast part of your operation also?"

*"Negative. They're part of a separate salvage operation diving on a shipwreck. You'd have to ask them exactly what they're up to. Back to work here, good luck fishing. Catch a couple for me."*

Dane gave a pleasant sign-off and hung up the

radio transmitter. "They didn't say what kind of shipwreck they were diving or make any mention of treasure," Dane noted.

"Probably figured they'd told us enough. More than I would have guessed."

Dane agreed. "Here are our options the way I see them: One, we make a dive on the capsule tonight. Hopefully the TV crew takes a break at night, but we can't count on that since it doesn't get any darker three miles underwater."

Bones squinted through the binoculars' optics. "They don't show any signs of slowing down from this distance. I see cranes moving, work lights on…"

"Two, we see if we can stealth-board the ship, then steal the nuke when and if they bring it aboard. Let them do the work, we steal the spoils."

Bones made a face. "Sketchy, bro."

Dane nodded. "Or three, we check out what's going on over at the shipwreck salvage operation."

"What for?"

Dane shrugged. "Something to do while we decided which of the first two to do. Test out the gear on something not quite as critical."

"But the TV guys could see us doing that and then our cover's blown right out of the water."

"True. Just thinking through our options."

"The easiest thing would be if we dove on the capsule ourselves and plucked the nuke from it on the first dive."

"That does sound pretty easy. Night launch a submersible, dive three miles down, pick up a nuclear bomb inside a lost space capsule. Bring it back to the boat undetected." Dane rolled his eyes.

"Relatively easy. Would you rather scuba dive at night a half mile or so from our boat to theirs, climb aboard undetected, hide out until they raise the capsule. Somehow get what's inside it without them knowing and bring it back to our ship?" Bones returned Dane's eye roll with interest. "And checking out the shipwreck. That's probably the easiest, but it doesn't really help us achieve our objective."

"Right, so take a look." Dane pointed to a GPS display in the console. "We motor another quarter mile closer to the *Ocean Explorer* and then we go for it.

Bones nodded. "I'll head down and get things set up."

**A quarter-mile** from the *Science Channel* ship, Dane engaged the auto-pilot to keep the vessel in a fixed position. So far he still saw only the same two vessels, and no one had made any contact with him since the initial radio call from the *Ocean Explorer*. He stepped out of the wheelhouse and into the cool evening air. Looking out over the water, he was pleased to note that the sea was relatively calm.

He descended the short flight of stairs down to the work deck where he pushed open a door that led to a seafood processing area. Retracing the route Captain Epson had show him in port, Dane then opened what looked like the door to a walk-in freezer. Behind its doors, however, lay not an ice encrusted fish box, but a tightly wound spiral staircase leading down. He descended the ladder-like structure, clutching the rail for support against the motion of the boat until he came out on a flat area belowdecks.

Well lit by ceiling mounted fluorescents, the space offered no view to the world above—no portholes, skylights, or doors. It did offer a different kind of view, however, and that portal dominated the center of the veiled space.

Known as a "moon pool," the unique vessel design featured a circular hole cut directly in the boat's hull, through which the ocean was directly accessible. The bottom of the pool could be sealed with a door while underway, and the sides of the pool protruded into the vessel in an extended lip. Dane heard the lapping of water against steel as he strode toward the watery aperture.

Bones was already here, fussing over the centerpiece of the room: a two-person submersible suspended from a crane a few feet above the water that swayed slightly within the moon pool's perimeter. The words *Deep Black* were stenciled inconspicuously on the black metal undercarriage that supported the cabin.

"Check out our sweet new ride," Bones said.

"The name fits. What do you think of her?" Dane asked as he walked over to the moon pool.

"It's a lot like the one we trained on." Bones rapped his knuckles on the underwater vehicle's clear dome. "It does have something a little extra, though." He pointed underneath the sub's belly. The feature was out of sight from Dane's vantage point, but because of Epson's tour, he had a pretty good idea of what it was.

"Weapons package?"

Bones grinned broadly. "We've got a six-pack of

short-range, underwater-to-underwater missiles."

"How about the manipulator arms?" Dane asked, wanting to deflect discussion of possibly having to use the craft's lethal weapons against a ship full of clueless science and history buffs.

"Both grab-arms checked out perfectly. I could lift a girl's skirt like that." He snapped his fingers.

"Please don't."

Dane circled the sub, appraising the craft that would take them three miles below the ocean, the machine upon which their life and mission success would depend. They went through a thorough checklist of safety related items, checking battery charge states, oxygen tank levels, carbon dioxide scrubbers, fire extinguishers and so forth. Once these checks were satisfactorily completed, Dane climbed into the pilot's seat.

"Ready?"

"Let's take her for a spin." Bones moved to the crane that would lower the sub into the moon pool. He operated the crane's controls to slowly lower the sub to the surface of the water. "Would be nice to have more crew at a time like this. It's not like we're getting paid by the hour."

Bones released the sub from the crane. Normal operating procedures called for both of them to be inside the sub when it was dropped from the crane, with the hatch closed. But the high degree of secrecy surrounding their mission meant that they would have no support personnel, necessitating a riskier launch.

"Well, it's just us. Don't rock the boat too much

when you drag your big butt onboard, or we'll have to phone the Admiral that we sank the nifty little spy sub he gave us."

Bones grimaced at the thought. He went to the edge of the moon pool and pulled the craft to him with a rope. He gingerly stepped aboard, wasting no time settling into his co-pilot seat where his weight would be properly distributed. Then he reached up and drew the acrylic dome hatch down over them, taking comfort in the familiar pressure against his eardrums as the bubble was sealed.

Dane immediately vented the buoyancy tanks and brought the sub straight down to avoid banging into the edge of the moon pool before they were below the boat's hull. He looked up once from a depth of one hundred feet and saw the warm glow of the boat's open underside. Below them lay only darkness.

Dane poised his hands on the controls. To conserve battery power on the three mile trip to the seafloor they would simply sink under force of gravity, with most of the sub's systems powered off. "About to shut off all non-critical systems. You good?"

"Always. You got the radio patch set up?"

If anyone hailed the *Atlantic Pride* on the marine radio while they were in the sub, it would seem strange not to respond, and could draw increased scrutiny. Dane tapped the sub's radio.

"If we get a radio call topside, we'll be able to respond from down here without anyone being the wiser."

"Kind of reminds me of forwarding work calls to a home number without telling the boss you won't be coming in that day."

Dane grinned as he consulted his sonar display and the two SEALs plummeted toward the bottom of the ocean.

# CHAPTER 5

**Three hours later**, Dane fully activated the sub's technology in preparation for reaching the bottom. Bones flipped on the external lights. A white, disc-like deep sea fish, trailing bioluminescent tendrils passed close by their viewing dome. The unearthly pressures at these depths weighed heavily on the minds of both men.

"Five hundred twelve feet to bottom." Bones eyed his instrument displays.

"We should be in the neighborhood of the capsule." Dane pulled back slightly on the joystick, adjusting their angle of descent. Although they began the dive a quarter-mile from the *Ocean Explorer* they had by now closed that distance due to the slight angle of descent that Dane had maintained by setting the craft's rudder against the prevailing currents and keeping a close eye on the compass.

"Two hundred two feet," Bones warned. Were the sub to actually hit the seafloor, in addition to suffering possible damage to the craft, they also ran the risk of stirring up the fine silt on the bottom that would ruin their visibility for hours—all the time they had on this dive. Dane was well aware of the fact that even several feet above the bottom, the prop wash from *Deep Black's* thrusters alone could stir up that silt. He slowed their rate of descent and leveled out the craft.

Although pitch-black, the water clarity at this tremendous depth was impressive. Dane had no trouble discerning in crisp detail whatever fell within the path of Bones' floodlights and searchlight. He peered down on a featureless mud plain, dotted with a few starfish and simple creatures that were unknown to him.

"They were right about the seafloor topography in the briefing," Dane said.

"Doesn't get any flatter than this," Bones agreed. "But I don't see any capsule, do you?"

Dane consulted the compass and made a slight course correction. "We're heading toward the expedition ship's position. We'll find it."

Yet an hour passed and still they had encountered nothing man-made. Dane warned Bones that they had another hour of bottom time before they would need to begin their return trip to the surface. The sub's power and oxygen supply would only last so long, and neither of them even wanted to entertain the notion of being stuck on the bottom three miles underwater with no power, completely in the dark.

Bones continued sweeping his search beam out past the swath of light cast by the floodlights while Dane took them closer to the *Ocean Explorer*.

"Dude, do you see that?" Bones cried.

Dane's head was suddenly on a swivel and his heart raced. "What is it?"

"An old Bud can. Like, from the 1950s. Mint condition too!"

The sudden rush of tension drained from Dane's neck and shoulders. "Low oxygen content down here, so the oxidation process is super-slow."

"You can't help it, can you?"

"What's that?" Dane cocked his head.

"You take something cool and turn it into a science lesson. No wonder your game is so weak with the ladies." Before Dane could reply, Bones continued. "It bodes well for us. Maybe the capsule is in good shape, including the nuke inside."

Dane nodded. "The few promo pics from the expedition they showed us in the briefing looked like the outside of the capsule, at least, was very well preserved. Hopefully, we'll find out soon."

Ten more minutes elapsed without sighting anything noteworthy.

"You sure that compass is accurate?" Bones glanced down at the display, a trace of nervousness in his voice. The featureless seafloor, in blackness beyond the radius of the sub's light arrays, would be an easy place to get lost, like wandering an endless expanse of desert sand.

"It's accurate." Dane tapped the navigation aid with a finger. "I think we've passed underneath the salvage ship and are now on the other side of it relative to our boat. The capsule is probably…" Just then, something caught his eye. "I see it!"

"Dude. Turn it down." Bones rubbed his ears and grimaced in mock pain.

Dane chuckled. The extra volume was completely unnecessary in the confined space, but after the monotony of the muddy bottom, the protuberance at the edge of his illumination field was worthy of emphasis.

There, resting on the bottom like some forgotten

child's toy, lay the *Liberty Bell 7*.

"Adjusting course." Dane maneuvered their agile craft toward the object of interest, careful to maintain a safe distance above the bottom. The only sound was the whir of the sub's electric thrusters while both operators contemplated the significance of this sighting. If they were in fact coming up on the sunken spacecraft, then things were looking good for their mission timetable.

They neared the hazy form. It loomed out of the flatness, shaped like a bell but canted to one side. Then Bones shone the search beam directly on the thing and they saw it: a white zig-zag of a line painted on the object.

"Hello *Liberty Bell 7!*" Dane said.

Bones stared at the lopsided cone. "Honestly, I was more impressed by the beer can."

Dane slowed the sub and hovered ten feet above the fallen spacecraft. "Let's get to work. Let me know when you're ready for me to move in."

"I'll take a radioactivity measurement to confirm the nuke is still on board and still active." The sub was outfitted with an external Geiger counter, and Captain Epson had given Bones a crash course in its use. Bones' practiced button pushing translated to smooth movements of the articulated arm outside the sub, and in short order he received a reading.

"Whoa, it's hot down there! Showing a lot of millisieverts. Way above normal background levels."

Dane took an extra moment to make sure the sub was under complete control. This was the real deal. The bomb was in there, all he had to do was keep the sub steady for Bones to pluck it out. "All right. You ready, Bones?"

Bones took a minute to test his grab-arms. "Ready. Work your magic, Ice Man."

"So does that make you Maverick?" Dane peered intently over the sub's control console as he spoke, finessing the joystick in order to bring the sub smoothly alongside the space capsule.

"No, I hate Tom Cruise. Should we drop in on it now?"

"Negative Ghostrider, the pattern is full."

"Now you're just making it weird, Maddock."

"Whatever," Dane said. "Keep an eye out for the hatch with the blown cover. That's most likely the only opening in the craft's hull."

Bones directed the high intensity beam along *Liberty Bell 7* as they circled it from a short distance above. "There it is!"

They looked down on a smallish rectangular opening in the spaceship. Dane guided the submersible through a series of incremental maneuvers until they were at eye level with the open hatch. Pillows of silt wafted from the bottom.

"Can you see in there?" Dane asked.

Bones pressed a rocker switch to move the search beam so that its light was cast inside the capsule.

"There's some crap scattered on the floor, but everything looks to be in pretty good shape."

"Crap? Can you elaborate?"

"There's a bar of soap. You know, like one of those little motel soaps that I always steal. Or take with me, it's really not stealing, right, if you're staying…"

"Bones! Stay focused."

"Okay, but there's something else…something shiny… Looks like a small metal square thing on the floor of it."

"Equipment that broke off?"

"It sort of looks like a box. If I can scoop it up we'll know for sure."

"If you can do it quick. We need to get a move on." Dane tapped their battery gauges.

"I see the nuke! Cylinder shape, maybe a foot long, just like they said."

"Why not just grab it so we can scoot?" For Dane, keeping the sub perfectly positioned above the capsule, battling the micro-currents, was a stressful task.

"It's a really small opening. I think I should practice with something non-critical first. I'll use the magnet attachment on the small manipulator arm so that I can snatch up that box. Once I do that I'll have the feel for it and go back in for the nuke."

Bones pressed a button to retract a metal cover that exposed a magnetic surface on the end of the grab arm. Then he operated the videogame-like controls that extended the arm in through the hatch opening to the interior of the space capsule.

"I'm in…" He positioned the arm over the box and lowered the magnet-containing claw to the capsule floor. A puff of silt billowed around the mechanical arm. Then he raised the arm, box attached, and retracted it back through the open hatch, ensconcing it safely inside the sub's tool bay.

"I *was* always good at those claw grabber games."

"Yeah, yeah, you just won the little cheap toy. Now go for the big stuffed animal to make your date really happy."

"We haven't been at sea long enough for you to start looking good." Like a dentist requesting drills from an assistant, Bones brought out the manipulator with the largest claw.

"This looks like it'll do." In the briefing, no one knew the exact dimensions of the nuke. That data had been lost to the ravages of time. "Too bad they couldn't make a specially fitted claw for this thing."

"You're a SEAL. Improvise."

"How do I make this thing flip you off?"

"Hold on," Dane said. An upwelling of water lifted their craft, and he took a moment to correct their position. "Okay, resume operations."

"Going in." Bones extended the manipulator arm to full length until it passed through the craft's open hatch. Dane's hand rested on the sub's control joystick, positioning the craft over the capsule like a hummingbird on a flower. Bones rotated the claw arm.

"I'm over the nuke. Making a grab for it."

Dane realized he was holding his breath as Bones brought the grasping tool over the cylindrical device and pressed the button that retracted its claws. They closed around the cylinder and Dane clenched his fists, as if in support. Bones gave the arm a tentative lift, saw that it held.

"I have it. Are we steady, Maddock?"

There was a two second pause while Dane confirmed his position relative to the capsule.

"Yeah." The word came in an exhale of breath and draining adrenaline.

"Withdrawing the arm with the package…here it comes… I'm just inside the hatch…"

Suddenly a brilliant light appeared out of nowhere in the darkness above and in front of them.

"We've got company! What is that?" Dane asked. "Not one of your contraptions, right?"

"Negative." As they watched, the light expanded through their bubble window, homing in on them.

"Another sub?" Dane queried.

"No, it's an ROV.  Autonomous, too, since it's got no tether. They sent a robot down here." Bones sat up straight, the usual glimmer of mischief gone from his eyes. He was all business. "And it's heading our way."

# CHAPTER 6

**"They must be** watching us through that thing." Dane kept his eyes locked on the remotely operated vehicle as it approached their mini-sub. "It's time to split. You have the nuke?"

The remote-controlled robot halted its forward progress near the perimeter of *Deep Black*'s floodlights. It hovered there, looking for all the world like a mechanical sentry who came across an intruder and now awaited instructions on how to proceed.

"Let me get the other arm around it."

A flash of light pierced the darkness.

"Is that thing taking our picture?" Bones asked.

"Looks like it." Dane frowned. What was going on?

"Must be the TV people. And I totally forgot to put on my makeup."

"I don't know." Dane watched as the ROV barreled toward them, chewing up the intervening space at a rapid clip. "I think they're trying to ram us."

"What the hell would they do that for?" Bones growled.

"I don't know. Just get a grip on the nuke."

"I've got it! Go!" Bones yanked the joystick back at the same time as Dane kicked the thrusters on full, sending the sub shooting upward.

"Son of a…!" Bones left his phrase unfinished as he let his head slam back into the co-pilot seat's headrest.

"What is it?"

"The nuke hit the side of the hatch when you put the pedal to the metal. It got knocked loose." He paused. "I dropped it."

"Did it land inside or outside the capsule?" Dane would have preferred it landed outside, since that way it had a chance of being covered by silt and overlooked by the *Science Channel* expedition. Also, it would make for an easier grab when they went back.

Bones leaned forward against the dome, shielding his eyes against the intruder's piercing spotlight that it leveled at them. "It fell back into the capsule."

Dane only exhaled sharply in reply.

"At least it didn't explode, right?"

"Tell that to the Admiral."

"He'd probably prefer that it exploded." Bones turned and saw the ROV skirt past the spacecraft and adjust its attitude upward.

"Hey, that spybot's still chasing us."

Another white flash invaded their cabin.

"It's trying to take a picture of our license plate, I guess," Dane said, aiming their sub almost vertically.

"We could test out the weapons system on it." Bones eyed the missile pod control assembly, a gleam in his eye.

"Not unless they shoot first or try to disable us in some way."

"Screw them. Let's go back down for the nuke and hope they try something. I'm in the mood to kick some ass."

Dane glanced down at the battery display. "No can do. We took too long searching. We'll be lucky to get back to the surface within a safe range."

"Well then I've got a Kodak moment for it." Bones raised both middle fingers in a double salute.

Dane only shook his head as he increased thruster speed to maximum, rocketing them toward the surface. Standard ascent procedure called for the proper amount of sub's ballast, lead weights, to be jettisoned, causing the craft to float gently to the surface. Dane knew, however, that although the bends, a scuba diver's malady that arose from ascending too rapidly, was not a concern for them in the mini-sub, that they would run their battery bank down before they reached the surface at this rate. Also, he knew that an ascent from depths such as these could spin out of control as it gained speed and buoyancy when the water became shallower. He had no desire to go end over end before rocketing through the surface out of control, creating a spectacle for whoever happened to be watching topside.

"Wonder how long til E.T. heads home?" Dane said.

Bones shrugged. "Beats the hell out of me. I'm more of an ALF guy."

Far below them, the ROV had ceased its pursuit and now circled *Liberty Bell 7*.

Dane eased up on the throttle and leveled the submersible. After a last look below, he dumped the some of the sub's ballast and they began to rise faster. He eyed the compass and gave the thrusters a burst to set them on a course toward their support vessel.

Bones softly pounded his fist into his hand. "I can't believe I dropped the freaking thing. Now I've got to sit here for two and a half hours and think about it."

"Things happen." Dane shared Bones' frustration. Had he made the right decision? Could they have gotten away with firing on the ROV? Should they have taken one more crack at the nuke before ascending?

A call came through, rocking him out of his dark thoughts.

"*Research vessel* Ocean Explorer *to fishing vessel* Atlantic Pride: *We require your assistance. Do you copy?*"

Dane made eye contact with Bones before picking up the radio transmitter. Did they know what was happening? "*Ocean Explorer*, this is *Atlantic Pride*, we copy, over."

"*Roger that,* Atlantic Pride. *Can you do us a quick favor and tell me if you see any ships off your port bow? You're blocking our view a little bit, and our radar's been a bit wonky today.*"

Dane talked off-air to Bones. "They want to know if there's a ship on the other side of us they can't see that might have deployed a mini-sub."

"Tell 'em we saw one but it's gone now. Throw 'em off the trail a little." He grinned mischievously.

Dane raised his eyebrows and spoke into the mic. "Sure thing. There is a vessel maintaining position off our bow but maybe a little bit to port." Dane mouthed the words *treasure hunters* to Bones.

"Roger that, *Atlantic Pride*, we see them. Anybody else, farther away than that?"

"Negative. Not right now. About an hour ago we

saw a ship to port but haven't seen it in a while." Bones gave him a thumbs up.

*"Copy that, thank you, signing off."*

Dane and Bones completed their uneventful return to the surface in silence. When Dane spotted the glimmer of their vessel's moon pool, he slowed their ascent and they surfaced inside the watery opening.

Bones opened the dome hatch and was about to exit the submersible when they heard the sound of a single person clapping, followed by a deep voice emanating from somewhere within the shadows of the moon pool area.

"Congratulations, you found it!"

# CHAPTER 7

**Dane's first instinct** was to reach for his SEAL-issue Beretta M9, but although he and Bones had one on board the trawler, all the way up in the cockpit, he had foreseen no need for guns aboard the tiny submersible. He watched Bones' frame go rigid as the Indian no doubt experienced a similar regret. Dane did have his dive knife on a sheath attached to his calf, but as they searched the shadows the figure of a man stepped into the light out from behind the crane.

He pointed a compact submachine gun Dane recognized as a TEC-9 in Dane and Bones' direction, sweeping the muzzle back and forth between the two SEALs.

"Hands in the air! Both of you. Tall guy, don't take another step. Sub pilot, you can stay put with your hands where I can see them."

Dane and Bones complied. Dane made a mental note never to be without his sidearm again while out on a mission. Not that he would have had a chance to use it so far, with the intruders' shocking element of surprise, but still. He'd feel a hundred percent better if he had it on him.

"What's the problem?" Dane asked.

"You from that *Science Channel* expedition?" Bones followed up.

It was either that or the treasure hunters, since

they'd seen no other craft.

"Don't worry about it." The man paused, his eyes taking in Bones' full height and breadth of shoulder. "You are, without a doubt, the biggest damn Indian I've ever seen."

"I'm big in a lot of ways. Ask your old lady."

The man chuckled.

"Who are you?" Dane kept his voice level.

"You can call me Streib." He gestured with the TEC-9 to Bones. "Here's what I want you to do, Tonto. Use the crane to lift the sub out of the water."

Bones moved his eyes without turning his head to look at Dane. He wasn't much for following orders in any situation, and now, even with a gun trained on him, the idea of executing an operation involving the sub without an okay from its pilot seemed to run counter to the big man's instincts.

"Do it," Dane said.

"Slowly," Streib cautioned.

Bones reached out to the button that would raise the crane arm. He pressed it and a mechanical hum filled the air as the submersible was pulled from the moon pool, water cascading from its hull.

"Stay where you are. Both of you." Streib approached the sub, his finger still firm on the trigger of the TEC-9. He strode up to the edge of the pool.

Dane could see now that Streib was a beanpole of a man with pale skin and wispy black hair fashioned into a bad comb-over. He wore a leather jacket over jeans with a pair of rubber work boots, and a small utility belt with a holster for the Tec-9, and several smaller pouches that Dane supposed might contain things like a knife, flashlight, perhaps a radio or satellite phone.

Streib crouched and stared intently at the area of the sub that housed the grab arms and sample collection bays. He swept his weapon at Bones, to make sure he remained compliant, and then back to Dane, where the barrel lingered.

"Extend the manipulator arms."

"That's my department," Bones interjected, earning another wave of the gun.

"You may tell him how to do it if he does not know how. Otherwise, just stand there and keep quiet."

Dane reached across the cockpit to the co-pilot area and pressed a button in full view of the attacker. They heard the revving of servo-motors and then a long shaft of steel protruded from the spherical craft, its metal grasping claws clutching nothing.

"Show me the other arm."

Dane extended the smaller manipulator appendage. The box stuck to the magnetic plate on the end of it captivated the trespasser's attention.

"So you found them!" Streib asserted loudly, his face contorting into a mask of disbelief.

"Found what?" Bones asked.

"Bring me the box." Streib shook the TEC-9 in Bones' direction.

Dane brought his right hand, still resting on the manipulator controls, down and slightly to the left where he deftly flipped open a plastic switch cover.

Bones moved to the grab arm and plucked the metal box from its magnetic plate. They heard objects rattling around inside.

"Open it and bring the coins to me."

"Let's see if you're right," Bones said. He opened the box, the hinges creaking as he raised the lid, and looked inside. "Well I'll be..."

"I said bring them to me!"

Bones walked the box over to Streib, who knelt, scooped a handful of silver coins out of the box, and placed them in his pocket. He handed the empty box back to Bones, who shook his head, walked back to the sub and put it inside the sample bay.

Streib looked up from examining one of the coins, his gun still aimed at Bones. "Now…"

Streib never got to finish his sentence. Dane punched the exposed button. Immediately they heard a high-pitched, energetic whine, followed quickly by a dull *whump*.

The gunman's face erupted into a grimace of terror and confusion.

One of the missiles rocketed past his head where it slammed into the steel doorframe of the moon pool's inner airlock. The explosion was instant and brutally powerful. An invisible fist struck them all a vicious blow as a wave of heat swept across them. Bones and the intruder were both knocked off their feet by the blast, while Dane sat suspended in the submersible, now twirling slowly in the air.

Bones recovered first from the blast and leapt to his feet. He reached the attacker in three strides, zeroing in on the hand still weakly clutching his weapon. Bones batted the weapon aside, wrapped a meaty hand around the man's wrist, and drove his knee into the man's exposed groin. As the fellow doubled over, Bones followed up with a knee to the forehead that sent the fellow to the ground on legs suddenly turned to rubber. He kicked the hand holding the gun hard with his rubber fishing boot, eliciting a grunt of pain and sending the firearm skittering across the deck far out of reach.

The intruder recovered enough to struggle to regain his feet. Bones dropped on the intruder, putting him into a control hold, Dane leapt from the dangling sub. He hit the moon pool deck hard, rolled, and broke into a sprint as he came to his feet. He dashed across deck and picked up the TEC-9. He checked the clip, confirmed that it was loaded, and then walked over to Bones and the attacker, gun raised.

Dane motioned for Bones to move out of the way. His partner extricated himself from the man, giving him a final shove as he stood and backed away.

It was Dane's turn to give the orders. "On your feet, hands up."

Their attacker wobbled to his feet like a frat boy on Saturday night. "That was loud," he groaned. While Bones had been tested with various types of ordinance detonating in close quarters throughout BUDS school and knew what to expect, their would-be attacker had clearly been stunned by the experience.

"You'll have to speak up so I can hear you over the ringing in my ears," the man mumbled.

"Hands up!" Dane yelled.

The stranger complied, fingers trembling but hands held high.

"Bones." Dane indicated a coil of polypropylene

dock line nearby.

Bones grabbed it and was on the intruder in seconds, binding his hands behind his back.

"Let's try this again," Dane said. "Who are you and what do you want with us?"

The man took a deep breath. "My name is Roland Streib. I'm really not your enemy. You've got to believe me. I just didn't handle things the way I should have."

"Dude, you got that right." Bones folded his arms across his chest and fixed Streib with a cold stare.

"Tell us something we don't know, Streib." Dane twitched the TEC-9 at their captive.

Streib narrowed his eyes and went on. "I'm the project manager for the space capsule salvage operation, for the *Science Channel*." He paused, as if this credential might impress them in some way. He was met only by the stony stares of two naval warriors.

"That's crap," Bones said. "A TV guy carrying a TEC-9? No way." He freed his dive knife from its sheath. "Tell us the truth or I start cutting off the parts you aren't using at the moment." His eyes dropped to Streib's belt line.

Streib's eyes widened. "It's true! I swear! I borrowed it from an ex-military buddy of mine for this trip. We've had some anonymous threats about disturbing the past or whatever. Besides, I wasn't going to hurt you. I only wanted to scare you away from the capsule."

"Why?" Dane demanded.

"We're about to raise it, for one thing. We don't need any interference. But…" He trailed off, looking at the submersible.

"But what?" Dane pressed.

"I also wanted to see what you brought up. The coins. I tried but couldn't get my ROV far enough inside the Bell to get them." He stared at the manipulator arm with the magnetic attachment.

Dane followed his gaze while keeping the gun trained on him in a rock steady stance. "So what's the significance of these coins?"

Their captive managed a laugh. "You don't have to feign ignorance. Why else would you be going to all the trouble to dive on the thing if you weren't already in the know?"

Dane and Bones exchanged glances and Bones nodded. The meaning was clear. Dane could take first crack at extracting information from the captive— which in turn would become intel once they brought it back to the Admiral. If he failed, Bones would take over.

Dane considered the situation. Above all, he needed to maintain their cover. He disapproved of torture and he really didn't enjoy killing, but would have considerably less choice in the matter should Streib prove to be privy to their agenda. He hoped it wouldn't come to that.

"I have no idea what you're talking about. We did bring up that metal box, but we didn't know what was in it until you told us."

Streib snorted. "Give me a break. Why else would you be diving on the capsule if it weren't for the coins? There's nothing else of real value on *Liberty Bell 7*. It's a priceless piece of American space history, sure, but it's not like you could sell it. It's still government property that you'd have to turn over. Besides, if treasure was all you wanted you'd be on the Spanish frigate site, only a quarter mile from here."

Dane thought fast. Apparently this guy knew a lot about some coins in the metal box that Bones found, but nothing about the nuke on board the craft. Dane had to keep it that way.

"We wanted to dive the Spanish wreck, but there's already another ship on that site, so we thought we'd check out the capsule wreck as a pre-dive to test our systems."

Streib glanced at the submersible, its spinning arc now beginning to slow.

"Listen guys, I don't know who you are, but you don't fool me. There are only a handful of subs in the world capable of working at these depths." He stared into the sloshing moon pool. "You must be U.S. government: either employees, contractors, or possibly military," he said, casting a sidelong glance at Dane and his new TEC-9 with which he already appeared more than comfortable.

Dane felt his jaw start to go slack and he willed it shut. Even Bones glanced over at him for the first time since he'd started guarding Streib. But it was the expedition manager who filled the silence first.

"You can drop the pretenses. I know why you're here."

# CHAPTER 8

**When neither Dane** nor Bones spoke, Roland Streib elaborated at gunpoint.

"You want these coins for the same reason I do..." He glanced down at his pants pocket where he had dumped them before continuing. "To prove once and for all that the Mercury-Redstone 4 mission was a fake. A sham. Hoax. A wool-over-the-eyes stunt in an attempt to scare the holy Hell out of the Russians."

Streib's hands started to come down and Dane shook the submachine gun. Streib put his hands back up high.

Dane was concerned at how close the salvage manager seemed to be to his true objective. It seemed like the nuke was the only thing he wasn't aware of.

"Less worrying about who we are, more about answering our questions. Tell us about the coins. Why do you think they're so important?"

"Space lore has it that at least one roll of dimes, Mercury dimes, naturally, went aboard the capsule with Gus Grissom. Gus and a bunch of the other astronauts and mission personnel wanted to have a souvenir of their flight. Some common object that they could say has been to space after the flight, to show off to their friends or even sell later on. But of course, these supposedly space-flown dimes went down with the capsule when it sank. Gus reportedly screwed the pooch and blew that hatch by mistake, causing the Liberty Bell to flood."

"Reportedly?" Dane prompted.

"I say 'reportedly' because I believe that's another lie. The government was trying to cover up the fact that the capsule was sent to the bottom on purpose, to prevent evidence that it never went to space at all from being found."

Dane felt his skin begin to crawl. This guy knew a lot, yet was wrong on some key counts. Besides omitting the nuke, the capsule *did* fly in space, for fifteen minutes in a suborbital hop. At least according to his briefing. This guy was starting to sound like one of those conspiracy theory nutballs who claimed Neil Armstrong never walked on the moon, that it was all done on a Hollywood sound stage.

Streib continued. "That hatch took a lot of force to open. They didn't want it coming off by accident. Imagine if you could just elbow it the wrong way while you're in space, right? So it was designed to require a lot of applied force to open. In fact, technicians maintain to this day that the only way to open it was to hit it so hard that it would leave a bruise on your hand or wrist. And guess what? They checked Gus' hands after the mission. No bruises to be found."

"So he never opened the hatch," Dane said.

"No! But NASA and the Kennedy administration always maintained that he did. Even in the face of overwhelming evidence to the contrary."

"So what do the dimes have to do with that?"

"The dimes have special symbols carved into them."

The sound of water dripping from the sub was all they heard for the next few seconds while Dane and Bones wrapped their minds around what Streib was saying. To Dane, it was starting to seem more and more fantastical—this guy *must* be a conspiracy theory wackjob. But it was easy enough to find out.

"Bones, check out the dimes."

Bones glared once at Streib. "Reach into your pocket, *nice and slow*, and pull out a few of the dimes." Streib complied, holding a palm full of dimes out toward Bones, who plucked a couple of them from Streib's hand before stepping back.

Bones held one of the coins up to the fluorescent work lights. He squinted at the round disc in his fingers. He repeated the process with a couple more. At length he said, "They are dimes. In pretty good shape…"

As he flipped them over his face took on a puzzled expression. He held a few of the dimes out for Dane to see. Scratched into the face of the coins were in fact strange symbols.

Dane looked up to see Streib grinning at him. "How do we know that you didn't just drop these in the capsule yourself with one of your ROVs?"

At that moment they heard radio chatter burst from the overhead speakers. It didn't pertain to them, but it reminded Dane that, should someone call them, they were a long way from the bridge. It wasn't normal for a vessel this far out at sea to ignore radio calls. Dane saw Streib about to respond but cut him off. "Hold on. Let's take this party up to the pilothouse.

Bones, escort our guest, if you would, while I bring up the rear."

Bones nodded and put a firm grip on Streib's right elbow. They marched to the airlock door, where Bones temporarily let go of the marine salvager in order to turn the heavy valve wheel that unlocked the thick metal door. Dane kept the TEC-9 trained on him while they walked into the airlock. Bones repeated the process with the outer door and then the three of them passed out into the crisp, night air on deck.

Dane's head was on a swivel as he scanned the waters surrounding their boat for any signs that Streib had accomplices waiting. But he saw only an empty inflatable boat, tied alongside the *Atlantic Pride* amidships, on the side that faced away from the salvage expedition's ship.

"How long before your people miss you and the inflatable?" Dane asked Streib from behind as they walked toward the wheelhouse.

Streib visibly stiffened. "Not long at all," he managed.

Dane chuckled. This was of course the expected answer. In his place, he conceded, he'd say the same thing. No need to give the enemy plenty of time to interrogate you. Still, he wanted Streib on edge. "You sure you're not supposed to be on a sleep shift right now, and that's why you came over here alone? Maybe no one expects you back for a few hours?"

"Oh, no. I'll be missed anytime now, if I haven't already. They probably think I took the Zodiac out to do a little night fishing. Not unusual at all, as long as I come back."

Dane looked off their starboard rail and saw the converted yacht humming with activity. Men buzzed about various pieces of machinery like bees about a hive. He kept the TEC-9 to his left side in case they were being watched through binoculars.

The unlikely trio reached the stairs to the wheelhouse and climbed up. Dane guarded Streib with the gun while Bones opened the door. Inside, Dane waved the gun barrel at the co-pilot's chair and Streib sat. Bones told him to put his hands down and bound him with the rope to the chair. Dane briefly consulted the boat's instrument panel. Satisfied all was in order, he turned his attention—and the gun—back to Streib.

"Okay, so where were we?"

"You were asking if he might have dropped the dimes into the capsule himself," Bones reminded him.

"Right, you've been working this site for days. How can you prove that's not what happened?"

Streib shrugged as much as his restraints would allow. "It's well documented that a roll of Mercury dimes was brought aboard that spacecraft."

Bones nodded. "These are old. 1941. Why use such old coins?"

"It was a tradition to us the Mercury dimes. You know… Mercury dimes, Mercury capsule."

"Sweet," Bones said. "Made with silver back then, too. Maybe I should keep 'em."

Streib frowned.

"Let's just assume for a second that these dimes are genuine," Dane said. "How do they prove the mission was faked?"

Streib spoke as he watched Bones pull two of the dimes from his pocket and examine them closely. "I believe that the symbols are a coded message from the astronaut on board the crew capsule. I think he had second thoughts about his orders to fake the mission."

"A whistleblower?" Dane asked.

"Sort of, yeah. But not so publicly. Back then, with the Cold War backdrop, patriotism and nationalism ran very high. He didn't want to appear unpatriotic, but he wanted to the truth to eventually be known. Unfortunately, someone caught onto what he was doing because he, I'm talking about Gus Grissom, was later killed in an Apollo 1 launch pad fire."

Dane and Bones exchanged knowing glances. Grissom was the astronaut in the capsule according to their briefing. But no one had mentioned he'd later been killed.

"But that was just an accident," Dane said.

"Was it?" Streib managed a grin. "That would be one heck of a coincidence, and a bit of good fortune for a government that wanted to make sure he never let slip their dirty little secret."

A moment of contemplation passed while Bones asked, squinting at one of the dimes, "So how do you read these things? This one has what looks like a triangle with an X through it."

Streib shook his head. "I don't know yet. I was hoping to collect all of them myself, without even my own crew knowing, and then work it out in my private study back home. "Because if the capsule comes aboard my ship with them in it, it'll be too late. There are all kinds of people on board: crew assisting with preservation efforts, museum specialists-waiting to photograph and catalog every little piece of anything that comes out of that spacecraft."

"How about if we let you keep all of the dimes," Dane offered.

"In return for what?" Streib countered.

"You're not exactly in a position to bargain here," Dane reminded him. "How about in return for not killing you?" Not that Dane was so coldhearted, but there was no need for Streib to know that. The trussed salvager shrunk in his chair.

"In return for clearing us a window where we can dive without ROV interference. Can you do that?"

"And will you do it?" Bones added.

Streib appeared confused, looking from Dane to Bones and back again. "But, if you really don't want the dimes, then…what do you want? You don't work for the Russians, do you? I know they'd like to get their hands on this piece of early American space technology."

The wall of silence his question was greeted with was answer enough. They were saying nothing.

"If you want those coins, you make it so that we can dive uninterrupted on that capsule," Dane said. "We're not going to hurt it or take it. We just want to look around without being hassled, and then we'll be out of your hair." Bones nodded in agreement.

Streib suddenly lifted his head. "Okay, deal."

Bones stepped up to Streib and relieved him of the remaining dimes.

"But listen, there's something else you should

know," Streib added.

Dane raised an eyebrow at him in silence. Streib elaborated. "We have been detecting some weird signals down there. Total anomalies."

"What kind of anomalies?" Dane asked.

"Odd sonar signals and even audio transmissions. We think there's a Russian sub down there. Not a submersible," he clarified, "but a full-blown naval warfare sub, hunting for the capsule. That's why I asked if you were contracting for them. You sure don't seem Russian, but who knows if maybe they hire mercenaries these days. They're smart, they do what they have to do."

"Why would the Russians be interested in the capsule?" Dane asked.

Streib looked almost embarrassed as he struggled with the answer. "Aside from grabbing the entire capsule to stuff in some museum in Moscow as a kind of final Cold War triumph, the most reasonable explanation I can come up with is that they also want to find the dimes so they can decode the message and prove to the world that the U.S. mission was a fake, and so it was really they who won the space race during the Cold War."

Dane and Bones exchanged a knowing glance that Streib mistook to indicate they thought his suggestion was plausible.

"See?" he said. "It makes sense, doesn't it?"

Dane looked at their prisoner. "Absolutely. When can we do our next dive on the capsule?"

# CHAPTER 9

**"You really think** we can trust that dude?" Bones asked. Earlier they had released Roland Streib, who had boarded his inflatable boat and rode it back to his ship, tail between his legs. Then they had motored their own vessel farther from Streib's *Ocean Explorer.* They did not want to suggest any kind of collaboration between themselves and the television ship. They now floated near the Spanish wreck site, not far from the treasure hunter vessel they had sighted there before.

"A space conspiracy nut with a gun? What's not to trust?" Dane made a face. "He wants those dimes. If it's in his power to do what we asked, I think we can count on him."

"I wish there was a way we could verify what he was telling us. I don't know much about the early space program."

"You don't know much about any space program, do you?" Dane ribbed.

"Got me there."

Dane reached across the cockpit and pulled down the encrypted satellite phone given to them by Captain Epson.

"Epson said not to even bother using that thing unless we had the nuke in our possession," Bones recalled.

"He said not to call *him*, unless we had it. He didn't

say we couldn't call anyone else," Dane said, lighting up the handheld device.

"We sure as hell can't tell anyone about…"

Dane held the phone up, its digital display ready to dial. "Of course not. But like you said, we just want to know a little more about the space program. We can call someone who might be able to tell us about it at face value, without even mentioning we're on a mission."

"Like who?" Bones asked.

"Know any space buffs?"

"Nope."

Dane grimaced. "Me neither. Nor do I know any NASA guys."

"Who do we know that's just a smart guy, not in the military?" Bones asked, scratching his head.

The pair of SEALs thought about this in silence for a moment, until Dane pumped his fist in a gesture of triumph.

"Okay, he's ex-military, but what about Jimmy Letson?"

"Oh yeah, the guy who helped us out in Boston that time?"

Bones grinned at the memory of an adventurous search for a historical lantern.

"Right, the Boston Globe reporter, who's good with computers. He might know something, or at least be able to look it up." Dane pulled out his wallet and rifled through it, coming up with a folded sheet of paper full of phone numbers.

"The Maddock rolodex," Bones said. "Any single ladies on that list, or just dudes with computer fetishes?"

"Here it is." He hit the speaker phone button and punched in Jimmy's number.

"Pretty late," Bones said, glancing at a clock in the cockpit. "Hopefully he's a workaholic."

"He's probably up playing Dungeons and Dragons or hacking some network for kicks." They heard a high, nasal voice emanate from the sat-phone speaker. *"Jimmy here."*

Dane pictured the tall, wiry man with his curly brown hair, thin mustache and round spectacles. "Hey Jimmy, it's Maddock. Sorry for the late call."

*"Maddock. Let me guess, you need a favor and you need it fast?"*

Dane grinned at Bones. "As a matter of fact, I do."

*"You in Boston? Bottle of Scotch again?"*

"No, actually Bones and I are travelling right now, through Florida."

Jimmy sighed. *"That's too bad. Some friends and I are just starting a game of D&D. You've never tried out that dwarf warrior I rolled up for you."*

Bones guffawed and mouthed "geek" while Dane's face reddened.

"Yeah," he said, "anyway, we need to know some info on the Mercury era NASA space program." He explained that they heard there might be some dimes that were brought aboard the *Liberty Bell 7* capsule.

*"Yep,"* Letson replied. *"It was common practice, and still is, for astronauts to bring small, light, personal effects aboard so that they would have something that's been to space afterward. You didn't know that? I thought you were supposed to be*

*intelligent, at least by swabbie standards."*

Dane ignored the jibe. "But I have also heard that there were some strange symbols carved into the dimes. Any idea what those are about?"

There was a slight pause on the other end of the connection. *"Strange symbols, you say? What's so strange about them?"*

Dane looked at Bones, who was looking at one of the dimes closely. He showed it Dane, who leaned in to look at it while he spoke on the phone. "Not sure, really, but maybe shapes, like triangles."

*"Are they cast into the coins or were they carved later?"*

"Definitely carved in later. Directly over the head side."

*"Hmm. So one of the astronauts did it. In that case, obverse or reverse, I doubt the side means anything. You're reading too much into it, would be my semi-informed opinion."*

"How so?"

*"Put yourself in the shoes of a 1960's astronaut or mission support specialist. Space was very new. To be able to have a space-flown object of any kind was quite a bragging right, and potentially even valuable. So what they did was, everyone put in their dime to give to the capsule astronaut, Gus Grissom, on this particular mission if I'm not mistaken, and to make sure they'd get back their exact dime and not one that was substituted, they would carve their initials, maybe. Or if they feared being reprimanded for bringing a dime on without permission—space contraband, you know— and didn't want to be identified, they would simply carve a symbol on it, so later on they could say, 'Hey that one's mine, the one with the triangle.'"*

Bones shook his head and laughed quietly, muttering something about Streib.

*"What made you think it was something more than that?"*

Dane felt a tinge of embarrassment. "We spoke to a guy who said they might have some meaning, something about proving that the mission was a lie and a fake and how they never really went into space at all."

*"Ah, so you've had a run-in with a space conspiracy theorist!"*

"Well, this person seemed like they could be knowledgeable…"

*"Right up until the part about the dime symbols constituting a coded message?"*

"I guess so. This individual also seemed to think that the Russians somehow could have been interested in the dimes, if they did carry a message, which I guess they don't."

Letson's voice seemed to perk up. *"Well, now actually there might be something to that aspect of it. That's the thing about these conspiracy theorists. They tend to take two different issues and conflate them to create meaning that isn't there."*

Dane frowned. "So you mean the Russians *would* be interested in the dimes?"

*"What I mean is that the Russians would be interested in anything that proves the mission was faked in some way, or was somehow misrepresented, since it marked a pivotal moment in the early Cold War space race. But forget about the coins. There was a living, breathing person more than willing to talk. He was a backup astronaut for the Mercury-Redstone 4 mission who trained right alongside Grissom leading up to the launch. I forget the man's name. But he later became an outspoken opponent of NASA and was sued at one point, I believe, for violating confidentiality clauses related to the Mercury program."*

Dane and Bones traded glances, recalling the documents they had signed.

Letson went on. *"My point being that for anyone really interested, there's no need to puzzle over some scratched up dimes, if you could even locate them all—the capsule sank in the deep ocean, I believe—when you have, or at least had for many years, one of the astronauts more than willing to tell his side of the story. In fact…"* They heard Letson tapping on a computer keyboard. *"Hold on, here it is… Yes. I saw a news piece a year or so ago about how this Mercury astronaut said he was taking a trip to Star City, Russia to meet with Soviet space officials there."*

"And what happened in that meeting?" Dane wanted to know.

*"Nothing. The meeting never occurred. The guy was killed in a freak accident. It says here he was hit by a train, just a few days before he was to leave for Russia."*

"Who the hell gets hit by a train?" Bones said. "My cousin Elijah did, but he was drunk on really cheap moonshine…"

Dane waved him into silence. The gears of his mind were spinning fast. He recalled aloud how Streib told them that Grissom had been killed in a fire.

*"That's also true,"* Letson said. *"But again, it doesn't mean it wasn't an accident. Fires and rocket launches unfortunately go hand in hand. But there is something else that is a bit unusual about this particular period of the NASA space program."*

"I'm all ears."

Dane heard Letson clacking away on a keyboard before his voice returned. *"There are some back page reports of a Mercury-era plan to detonate a nuclear bomb on the moon."*

Dane was stunned for a moment but recovered quickly. "What's the point of bombing the little green men?"

*"You got me. But the thinking at the time was that it would intimidate the Russians as some kind of display of space weapons power. But keep in mind that this operation is pretty much just hearsay and was probably never run."*

"Weird." Dane ran a hand through his hair, mulling over this new information. "Well, I guess I'd better let you get back to your friends."

*"Are you kidding? I lied. I'm playing by myself. Besides, this is more fun. I might keep digging just for the heck of it."*

"In that case, I'll let you get on with it. You can call me at this number if you learn anything interesting. Thanks for your help."

*"You can thank me with drinks and a good meal next time you're in town."* In typical Jimmy fashion, he ended the call without saying goodbye.

Dane looked at Bones, who was flipping one of the dimes again and again.

"This," Dane began, "is turning out to be one weird mission."

**Dane climbed back** into the cockpit of *Deep Black* and ran through some diagnostic checks on the sub in preparation for another dive on *Liberty Bell 7*.

"What if Streib was lying about giving us a window to work alone down there, and he attacks us with ROVs?" Bones asked from his position at the moon pool crane.

In answer, Dane's arm reached across the

instrument console and the externally mounted missile pod swiveled in Bones' direction.

"Five left," Bones said, referencing the missile they used on Streib. He went to the same manipulator arm he'd grabbed the nuke with and fully examined it. Satisfied it was undamaged, he gave Dane a thumbs up and went to the crane.

"One way or another, we need to go back down there and grab that Cold War artifact," Dane said, looking up from the cockpit. "Space Boy said his team plans to attempt to raise the capsule later this afternoon, so we need to use this window to snatch the thing."

"Nothing else to do out here in the middle of the night," Bones said. He lowered the sub to the water with the crane and climbed into the co-pilot seat.

"So the plan is to drop down on the wreck site and then cover the quarter mile to the capsule on the seafloor. If we do that, according to Streib, we'll come up on the capsule shortly after their ROVs are called back to the ship for maintenance."

"And if anyone from the expedition has figured out that we have a sub, they'll think we're just diving for the treasure ship," Bones said.

Dane nodded in agreement. "Then we grab Little Fat Girl or whatever cutesy name somebody probably thought up for that A-bomb, and head for the hills."

He pulled the hatch over them and Bones latched it in place.

**Four hours later**, as dawn approached three miles above, Dane and Bones reached the seafloor once again.

"This looks sort of familiar, "Dane said, staring out at the featureless mud flat. "Having some real *de ja vu*, here, how about you?"

"I would be, if it weren't for this sonar reading I'm getting." He tapped a small screen with some squiggly yellow lines on it.

"How far out?"

"Maybe a hundred yards, dead ahead."

Dane locked their course into the sub's navigation system and they scooted across the deep sea plains toward the reading. A few minutes later a structure appeared out of the gloom.

"Spanish frigate," Dane observed, hovering the submersible a safe distance away and above.

The two operatives marveled at the pristine condition of the aged sailing ship.

"Thing is in outstanding shape," Bones commented, his eyes tracing the distinctive outline of the bow.

"Low oxygen content in the water down here preserves the wood."

"That means the crew…" Bones trailed off as he gazed at a ship more than a half millennia old.

"In there, maybe even with skin still on their bones," Dane said.

A soft beeping emanated from Bones' side of the cockpit, and the Cherokee focused his attention on one of the instruments in his charge.

"This is funny. I'm getting a reading on the Geiger counter."

Dane brought the sub in a smooth arc around the ship's broken forecastle, coasting over a debris trail that seemed to spill from the wreck. As he did, the frequency of beeps from the Geiger counter increased.

"What's so funny about that?" Dane said. Was it possible the Admiral and the General had not told them the complete truth regarding the role of nuclear weapons on the Mercury mission? They were, after all, only SEALs—tools of force used by the powers that be to carry out their directives. Dane was under no illusion that they were told nothing more than the bare minimum of what they needed to know in order to complete their objectives.

"We're way too far from the capsule to be getting a reading from its nuke," Bones stated matter-of-factly.

"Right, so does that mean there are more nukes that were dumped down here they didn't tell us about?"

Bones fiddled some more with the radioactivity meter's settings, alternately looking down on the debris trail and back to the Geiger counter's screen.

"Do me a favor and drop down a little closer to that field of rocks over there."

Dane eyed the rubble field and eased the sub closer to it. Bones' eyes were locked to his device display. "I think it's coming from those rocks."

Dane eyeballed the dull-looking stones skeptically. "You sure it's not from inside the wreck?"

Bones shook his head. "Readings get weaker closer to the shipwreck, stronger toward this trail of rocks."

"Maybe there's a device hidden under them?" Dane piloted the sub around the perimeter of the rocky pile.

"I think it's just the stones, dude. Readings are

pretty equal all the way over this mound. But I've got an idea."

"You've got an idea that doesn't involve either women or dive bars?"

Bones snorted. "Yeah, I guess I do. I say we take a sample of these rocks, check 'em out later back on board the boat."

"What for? We need to get over to…"

"Chill. It'll only take a couple of minutes. And look, these things look like they spilled out of the ship. A Spanish frigate was pretty much always a treasure ship, wasn't it?"

"I don't know. They don't look like gold or silver or anything valuable, really."

"Such a pessimist, Maddock. After five hundred years, they could be all encrusted over, couldn't they?"

Dane frowned. "But what's with the radioactivity? I guess we could collect some and show them to the wreck divers up there, but they'd probably just get into a territorial pissing contest with us."

"Enough with the thinking ahead. Let's just get us some and we'll figure out what to do with them later."

Dane dropped the submersible to within a couple of feet of the mound of rocks. Bones used the long grab arm to transfer a pile of the geological specimens into a collection box stored outside the sub.

"Happy?" Dane asked. He pressed a button and they heard the soft hiss of compressed air venting into the sub's buoyancy tubes. "These things are weighing us down. Let's head to the capsule."

"Always with the negatives."

Dane checked the compass and set off in the direction of the space wreck. They coasted across the bare seafloor, Bones occasionally spotlighting a strange denizen of the deep.

"Freaky down here, man. I hope we can grab that nuke this time so we can get back to base tomorrow. I got this chick's number and I was supposed to call her last night."

"I'll put you on the capsule, Bones. You just grab that thing."

"Slow out this time, too."

"You got it. No ROV is going to scare me this time, if we see it, I'll…"

"Whoa!" Bones interrupted him to point at his sonar display.

Dane turned his head sharply to look. He saw only an empty readout and Bones' confused face.

"What is it?"

"It's…gone."

Something in Bones' voice set Dane on edge. "What's gone?"

"I don't know. It was there for a second, I swear. A large signature, then it squiggled off the field."

Dane knew that as a sonar specialist, Bones had received specialized training in recognizing undersea sonar signatures. "Well, what was it?"

"It was big. Sort of looked like a…well never mind."

"No really, what did it look like?"

"Like a warfare-class submarine."

# CHAPTER 10

**Dane roved around** a tall stalk-like life form growing out of the bottom and lined up his compass course toward the capsule.

"Streib said something about the Russians," Dane said.

"Look, Maddock, I'm not sure yet, okay? It was only there for a second, and up a few thousand feet higher, too. I'm trying to remember all those signatures they showed us in training…" Bones rubbed his temples as if to coax the memories to the forefront of his mind. "It could have been a giant sea creature, an oarfish, maybe?" he hoped aloud.

"Don't worry about it for now. Whatever it was, you said it's up higher. I'll boost our speed a little so we get there faster. Let's do this thing." Dane put the submersible's thrusters on high and their craft accelerated over the deep mud flats.

Bones kept his eyes glued to the sonar monitor while they traversed the distance to the spacecraft, but the next thing to show up on his display was *Liberty Bell 7*.

"Capsule up ahead on the right," seventy-five yards," Bones said.

Soon they saw the looming form of the space capsule. Dane and Bones kept a sharp eye out for ROVs but for the moment, at least, they were alone.

"You know the drill," Dane said. Bones began testing the manipulator arm he would use to grab the nuclear bomb while Dane maneuvered the sub next to the tilted capsule.

"It's all good, ready when you are," he said, flexing his fingers in preparation for the precision movements he would need to perform.

"Copy that, moving in." Dane repeated the maneuvering he'd done on their first trip to the capsule, and in a few minutes he had the sub hovering once again over *Liberty Bell 7*'s open hatch.

Bones aimed the external spotlight into the sunken space relic, probing for the bomb. The sub lurched and they almost knocked into the capsule, but Dane corrected for the movement with a quick burst of reverse thrust.

Bones looked his way. "What's up?"

"Sorry, got caught in some kind of downwelling. Weird. It's been totally calm down here until now."

Bones turned back to the window, peering inside the capsule. For one heart-stopping moment he thought the nuclear device was no longer there, but then he spotted the cylindrical form.

"There it is! It's to our lower left." He pointed. "I'll need to come in from higher and to the right."

Dane positioned the craft accordingly and Bones aimed his light again.

"Better?"

"Good as it gets," Bones said, already priming the grab arm. "I'm going in."

Dane kept his hands poised and ready over the sub's controls, giving brief bursts of thrust every few seconds in order to maintain position.

They heard the mechanical whirring of the specially outfitted manipulator arm as Bones extended it into the downed spaceship. Dane could hear the Cherokee SEAL mumbling unintelligibly as he concentrated on dropping the claws around their prize. Then he heard Bones curse, mumble some more, followed by, "Got it! Do not move the sub!"

Dane complied while Bones withdrew the arm until the nuke was clutched in front of the open hatch. There, he turned the arm to orient the nuke so that it would fit through the opening. He retracted the grab arm.

"It's out!"

"Do you drop it in a sample box or keep it in the grabber?"

"Box. In case we lose momentary power to the arm and the grabber releases. And so no one can see it when we surface."

"I'll hold position while you park the car in the garage."

Bones opened the sample bay on the outside of the sub. He had just started moving the manipulator arm toward the box when they saw lights from above.

"Bones, is that your spotlight?"

Bones did not look up from his controls. "Negative."

"Then we've got company again. Looks like Streib lied to us. When I get hold of him this time, I'm…"

Suddenly the light shining on the seafloor next to the sub began strobing, lending a surreal quality to this underwater world, as if Dane was watching a very old silent film. He squinted against the flashes.

Bones shielded his eyes with the hand not on the controls. "Deep sea disco time."

"That strobe is disorienting. I need to go before I knock into the capsule. You got the nuke?"

Bones pressed a button with a flourish. They heard the sample bay door click into place. "We got it, man!"

"Say goodbye to Liberty Bell 7." Dane pulled the joystick all the way back and the sub pointed toward the distant surface. He activated the thrusters and Deep Black shot upward.

"Watch out!" Bones warned. But it was too late.

The impact was sickening— a jarring crunch to the top of their acrylic dome—the only thing separating them from the bone-crushing pressures of the deep ocean.

"What is that?" Dane yelled. But as he craned his neck to look up, he had his answer before Bones said, "Submersible."

Dane executed a downward thrust maneuver that should have sent the sub skittering back to the bottom. But instead he only heard the grinding of metal on metal. He tried the controls again to no avail. So focused was he on this effort that he almost didn't register the meaning of what Bones had said.

"Did you say submersible? Not ROV?"

"Yeah! I'm looking up at a mini-sub with two dudes in it! One of them has got us snagged in his grab arm."

"Is it Streib?" Dane's fist clenched as he suddenly imagined breaking Streib's jaw.

"Nope. Never seen 'em before. White dudes, military haircuts. And they look pissed off."

Dane again tried a combination of control jockeying that turned out to be futile. "Damn! No good."

"Maybe someone is after this nuke after all," Bones said, still looking up at the undersea craft they grappled with. "The capsule's down there, free for the taking. But they want us."

"Do you think they saw you grab the nuke and put it into the hold?"

"No way. I'm sure it was in before they got close enough." Bones suddenly snickered, reading some perversity into the words.

Dane scowled. "Let's get back to our boat and then we'll pay a little visit to Streib's ship."

Bones looked up at the sub, now deploying a second grab arm onto *Deep Black's* metal framework. "Uh, sure, there's only a couple of tons of submersible Transformer standing in our way. Maybe if you said 'Simon Says?'"

"What about our missiles?"

"We'd blow ourselves up right along with them because they'd detonate so close to us. I was hoping this mission would be a blast, but not that much of a blast. So now what? They're pushing us back down."

Dane consulted their depth meter and saw that Bones was right. Slowly but certainly, they were being forced back to the bottom.

"Point the spotlight up at them, at least. Make it harder for them to see us."

Bones aimed the powerful halogen straight up into the cockpit of the marauding mini-sub. He saw the pilot reflexively shield his eyes with a hand.

"Check out the look on his face!" Bones exclaimed. "It's like when a chick sees you naked for the first time."

"Get serious for a half a second, will you?"

"Don't sweat it. I'm a multitasker."

"Whatever. Maybe we can make radio contact?" Dane knew that undersea radio communication from sub-to-sub was tricky business, and judging by the look on Bones' face, he did as well.

"Might as well give it a shot. If they're transmitting to their support ship we might be able to hear that, too."

Dane attempted to extricate their craft from the newcomer's claws while Bones scanned available radio frequencies. They were hearing a lot of static and squelch noise until suddenly, human voices erupted in the cabin.

Dane looked up from his controls.

"That's not English," Bones said.

They heard more of the chatter, one of the parties sounding far away, one loud and clear. "...*nyet*..."

"Russian." Dane's stomach did a flip-flop. The mission was in a serious downward spiral at the moment.

"Talking to their support ship." Bones adjusted the radio controls. "Should I break in?"

"How's your Russian?"

"Uh, *vodka, Stolichnaya, Kournikova*—she's pretty hot, you know, um..."

"Okay, okay."

"I could try some Cherokee on them. I could accuse them of having marital relations with goats. My cousin's father in-law…"

"Just ask them in English what the hell they want."

Bones picked up the transmitter while the two locked subs continued to drift towards the bottom.

"Russian submersible: this is submersible *Deep Black*. Seems we've had a little fender bender. Please state your intentions, over."

Bones looked over at Dane, who nodded. "Good work. Keep it diplomatic if we can. Three miles underwater is no place for a fight."

"Especially holding onto an old A-bomb."

The radio reply that came commanded their attention, as much for the fact that it was in English as for the actual words.

*"Transfer the bomb to us and we let you go."*

# CHAPTER 11

**Dane and Bones sat** in stunned silence, processing the words they'd just heard while the two submersibles landed on the seafloor next to the space capsule. A cloud of silt billowed up around them.

"Tell them we don't know what they're talking about," Dane said. How did the Russians know about the bomb?

Bones picked up the radio transmitter and conveyed the message.

The response that came was English with a clipped Russian accent.

*"Our radiation detection equipment shows that you have the bomb aboard your craft. Do not lie. Pass it to us and we will go our separate ways."*

"Any luck breaking free from Hercules, here?" Bones asked, looking over at Dane, whose hands flew over the controls, trying different tactics, apparently none of them working.

"No. I can't see crap now," Dane said.

"At least they can't either."

"That could be a good thing!"

"What do you mean?"

Dane looked outside at the swirling maelstrom of suspended mud particles. "I think we try the old hidden ball trick."

Bones glanced outside the sub at the sample

collection bay where the explosive device sat. "Say what?"

"The hidden ball trick. Remember my old coach, Marco Cosenza? He taught it to me in Little League. It's basically the old bait and switch."

"Oh, yeah. What are you thinking?"

"You said those rocks we picked up from the treasure wreck gave off a radiation signature almost as strong as the nuke."

"Almost as strong as the sexuality I exude around the ladies." Bones smiled.

"So we drop the rocks here and they'll detect the radioactive reading from them on the bottom. Meanwhile we still have the nuke onboard."

"But that gives off a signature, too."

"They have no reason to suspect we're holding on to anything radioactive other than the bomb," Dane said. "I think if we just tell them *okay, we dropped it*, they'll do a reading aimed at the bottom and when they see it's positive they'll go to grab it. They'll have to release us in order to do that, and that's when we split for topside."

"I like it!"

"Better hurry. It's just our luck that there's a current running through here and I can already see the visibility beginning to clear." Outside, the black water was still a kaleidoscope of swirling particles and reflected light, but there were now pockets of clarity. Bones set to work opening the sample bay that held the rocks recovered from the shipwreck. They heard the electronic hum of the bay door sliding open.

"What if they hear that?" Bones worried.

"I'll mask it with lots of servo motoring and thruster application so they just think it's from our efforts to free ourselves," Dane said, hands throwing switches on the control board.

Bones went back to work. "Dumping," he said, peering into the black veil outside. He could just barely make out the sample bay where the rocks were.

"Hurry. It's clearing fast. If they see us messing with the bays they'll know we're up to something."

"Rocks are dumped. Bringing the bay back level…"

The radio boomed with the Russian voice. *"Do not waste your battery power trying to free yourselves. Give us the device and be on your way."*

"C'mon, Bones." Dane hit the thrusters some more.

"Closing bay door…It's shut! Bomb is in our hold, rocks on the bottom next to the capsule."

"Take a Geiger counter reading on the bottom to make sure it worked."

Bones pointed the radioactivity instrument's sensor where the rocks should be on the bottom. He consulted a display. "Yeah, nice and hot."

Dane picked up the radio transmitter and spoke into it: "Roger that, Russian submersible. We don't want any trouble. We have dropped the device, whatever it is, onto the seafloor next to the capsule, over."

The Russian accented transmission in response was immediate. *"We will remain engaged while we confirm your statement."*

"I usually make a guy buy me a drink before I let

him hold me this tight," Bones said.

Dane heard a small sound from the Russian sub that might have been a grunt of laughter.

A tense minute passed in the sub while they waited for an indication that their ruse had worked. Looking through the acrylic dome, Bones could now see the grab arms and payload bays , and was relieved to see the door concealing the nuke snugly shut.

"I don't know," Dane said. "They've had enough time to take a reading by now. Maybe we should ask them what's up."

And then they heard the faint mechanical whirring of their captors' manipulator arms just before their radio crackled with the Russian's voice.

*"You have been released. Leave the site immediately and do not return."* They felt *Deep Black* list to the right as it was ejected from the Russian sub's grab arms.

"Let's do this thing!" Bones shouted, but Dane needed no encouragement. He already had them off the bottom and ascending at an angle away from the submersible. In his haste to leave, his path took them closer than was comfortable to the space capsule. Bones' eyes widened as the words *LIBERTY BELL 7* filled their bubble view, and then they were clear, passing over the capsule and flying through the blackness.

"Yes!" Bones whooped.

"I can't remember when I've seen you this happy outside of a Hooters restaurant," Dane said, aiming their little craft upward while keeping one eye on the dashboard's instrumentation.

"We've got the bomb and they're stuck with those freaking rocks! I wish I could see their faces when…"

Bones' celebration was short-lived as he caught a shadow on his sonar readout in the corner of his eye.

"What is it?"

"I've got another sonar reading."

"Sub chasing us?"

Bones stared more intently at the display. "No…I don't think so. Because this reading is… above us."

Dane took a deep breath as he leveled out the sub, maintaining a constant depth. He leaned over to look at the sonar display. "That's a big signature, isn't it?"

"Huge." And then Bones' face twisted into a mask of concerned recognition.

"What is it?"

"I just remembered what this sig is from sonar school."

Dane stared transfixed at the elongated, fuzzy blob on the little screen. "And?"

"It's some kind of Russian naval submarine. Like Streib was saying. Not mini-sub, but full-on, nuclear-powered, bring-war-to-your-doorstep, don't-pass-go-don't collect-two-hundred-dollars Russian Navy submarine, probably Typhoon class." Dane was speechless, so Bones continued. "Underwater cruising speed of twenty-seven miles per hour. Can stay submerged for up to four freakin' *months*."

"Great," Dane managed. "Anything else?"

"Outfitted with hundreds of nuclear warheads."

The confines of the chilly submersible with its dry, recycled air and complex array of fragile life support systems suddenly verged on the claustrophobic for

Dane, but he relied on his SEAL training to call up reserves up endurance that the average person didn't know they could access. He'd been in sticky situations before.

"Let's just go up and around it, giving it a wide berth, and get back to the ship. They have what they want, or at least they think they do." He hoped the Russians didn't learn the truth before he and Bones were safely away.

"It's about 3,000 feet almost directly above us."

"I'll take us up at an angle so we go wide past it." He knew this was a temporary measure at best. If the Russians really wanted the bomb, they wouldn't give up the pursuit, and *Atlantic Pride* would afford them no refuge against a nuclear submarine. *One problem at a time*, he told himself.

Dane put the sub to full throttle and they ascended. After fifteen minutes he was starting to relax a bit when Bones pointed at the sonar display. "Multiple bogies! We have a contact right below us now, too."

Dane grimaced."How'd they sneak up on us?"

Bones shook his head. "Must be using some sort of sonar masking technology. Never seen it before on a submersible. They're used mostly for research and salvage, so almost always the operators want to be found by sonar."

Dane looked between his feet and was mortified to see the Russian mini-sub rocketing toward them. "I've got a visual. It's coming up fast, below and behind us."

"Just like a shark," Bones muttered.

"Which makes us the minnows." Dane gritted his

teeth and focused on the task at hand.

"How about we send a missile their way? I'm in the mood to blow some crap up."

"What's the point? With the mothership right up there, it could take us out anytime they wanted like swatting a fly."

Bones cursed. "So we just let them ram us? Damn, bro, that thing is *fast*."

A flood of light invaded their cabin and Dane tensed. "Brace yourself!"

For the second time on this dive they felt a jarring impact as the Russian submersible slammed into *Deep Black*. Bones picked up the radio transmitter.

"Now what?"

The action of metal claws grating on their sub's undercarriage vibrated beneath them.

The Russians responded. *"You tricked us with rocks. They must be uranium or plutonium ore. We do not know where they came from, but it is of no matter. The device is still on your craft. Our radioactivity readings confirm it."*

"It's just more of the rocks. That's all we have," Bones replied.

*"We must examine your craft to see if what you say is true."*

Bones looked over at Dane, who was fighting the sub's controls. "What is this, some kind of deep sea traffic stop?"

Dane shook his head. "Somehow I don't think they're going to write us a ticket and let us go. They're dragging us up now. Toward the submarine."

Dane applied their thrusters full force in the opposite direction from where the sub was pulling them but still their upward progress was inexorable.

Bones looked up through the dome, aiming the spotlight. "I see it! It's massive, man. They're…" He looked incredulously at the dark torpedo shape menacing above.

"They're what?" Dane never lifted his eyes from the control panel as he sought a piloting solution to their woes.

"They're opening a moon pool door in the hull! They're going to take us aboard."

# CHAPTER 12

**Dane glanced up** and saw the circle of light in the middle of the Russian submarine's underside. The submersible dragged them closer to it with each passing second.

"What's our next move, Maddock? Because I don't know about you, but if this is the invitation," he pointed to the assemblage of grab-arms towing them up to the warfare sub, "then I don't think I want to go to the party."

"Not looking forward to an evening with the comrades, eh?" Dane flipped various switches on the control panel, seeking actions that would free them from their aggressor.

"Somehow I don't think caviar and ice sculptures are what they have in mind for a couple of Navy SEALs caught lying about a Cold War A-bomb."

"It's our bomb," Dane pointed out. "They're the ones trying to steal it."

Bones looked up at the Typhoon class sub, the water in its moon pool shimmering under interior lights.

"Gee, why didn't I think of telling them that before?" Bones reached for the radio. "Maybe I'll just…"

Dane grabbed him by the wrist. "Take it easy. At this point they're not going to let us go. So we may as well think of our strategy for once we're prisoners of war."

"POWs? What war are you talking about? There's no war on right now!"

"Prisoners of the Cold War."

Bones' silence said volumes about the seriousness of the situation. As part of SEAL training, they'd had endurance sessions that would supposedly help prepare them, both physically and psychologically, for if and when they were ever captured and interrogated under duress or even tortured. But knowing that even the worst moments of those extreme preparedness sessions were administered by SEAL instructors, people who basically had their best interests at heart, couldn't possibly stack up to the real thing. And as the Russian mini-sub slowed in advance of reaching the Typhoon submarine, both Dane and Bones knew that this was indeed not a drill. They were miles beneath the ocean, their craft incapacitated by an enemy combatant.

Dane slipped a hand down to his waist where he felt for the lump of his Beretta in a holster beneath his sweater. Its bulk comforted him but he knew that he would need to conceal it better. Quickly he removed the holster and stashed it beneath his seat, keeping the gun in his back jeans pocket.

"We should split our guns up," he told Bones, who immediately ditched his holster as well to reduce bulk. "I'll try to hide mine on my person, in case they don't frisk us for some reason, but I think yours should stay hidden in here."

"Makes sense, I'll put it here," Bones said,

concealing his weapon in a compartment beneath the instrument cluster. "But I really don't see what two pistols are going to do against a full-fledged naval war machine, anyhow. They've already gotten the better of us just with their mini-sub," Bones reasoned.

"We've still got our missile pod with five left."

Bones checked the view of the pod outside the dome. "Looks like once again they've deliberately smothered it so that we can't fire them without blowing ourselves up."

"I don't suppose you can rig up a way to remote fire them? So when we're taken off the sub inside the big sub, we can cause a distraction?"

Bones looked at the firing mechanism on his side of the dash. He flipped open the protective cover and stared at the red button within a directional keypad. Then he looked over at Dane.

"You're the MacGyver, bro. I just know how to shoot the thing."

The two of them peered up into the moon pool of the Russian submarine, where they could now see indistinct silhouettes of people staring down at them.

"Remind me when we get back to tell the powers that be that we need a remote control for the missile pod."

"If we get back, I'll be happy to do that," Bones said glumly.

"I've got an idea," Dane said slowly, transfixed by something down on the cockpit floor.

"You might want to spit it out, because we're here." Bones looked up and saw the surface of the sub's moon pool mere feet away.

Dane knelt down and disconnected a gas hose, turning a knob on a tank and switching a flow valve.

"Yo Maddock, what're you doing with our oh-two?"

"If we flood our cabin with oxygen…"

"This thing'll be a bomb waiting for a spark!"

"Yeah. Such as from a bullet. But I don't think I need to remind you that's last resort only kind of stuff. This thing is our ride home. If it gets destroyed, we're totally dependent on the Russians to get back to our boat."

"I'm with you," Bones said, now waving at the stone-faced Soviets waiting around the moon pool.

"You don't happen to have your trusty butane lighter on you, do you?"

Bones shook his head. Normally he did carry one, but any kind of ignition source was strictly prohibited around submersibles due to the close proximity to pressurized pure oxygen.

"Okay, just put your hands up," Dane said, his fingertips touching the top of their cabin dome. Bones frowned but followed suit. "Always knew I'd go places with you, man."

*Deep Black* vibrated while a crane hook was latched on to their superstructure and the submersible holding them dropped away. Then they were lifted from the water through the moon pool, water sheeting off their dome, the view outside like that of looking out of a car while inside an automated carwash. Even with the distorted view, there was no mistaking the large hammer and sickle painted on the wall of the moon pool area.

"You know the Russian national anthem?" Bones asked.

Before Dane could answer, they heard the snapping of the dome hatch being undone from outside. Looking out at their new surroundings, Dane counted no less than six individuals wearing sailors' jumpsuits pointing a firearm at their submersible. Dane figured he had time for one last sentence to Bones without being overheard.

"Whatever you do, don't do anything to make them shoot us while we're near the sub remember?"

"Understood," Bones said as the dome hatch was raised and tilted back.

A squat, bald man built like a bullet took a step toward the sub, clearly regarding Dane and Bones with contempt. He asked them a terse question in Russian. When all he received in return were blank stares, he turned and nodded to one of his associates, grimaced, and switched to English.

"Identify yourselves."

Dane knew the fishermen cover wouldn't hold water. Fishermen didn't use submersibles. He had to think fast, and worrying about what Bones might be about to say wasn't helping his concentration. Nor was the assemblage of firepower aimed in his direction.

"We're part of a television network expedition to raise the American space capsule," Dane said, emphasizing the word *American* ever so slightly.

Bullet Man gave a sour grimace. "We have observed you via sonar returning in your submersible to the 'fishing trawler'," he countered, adding emphasis of his own. The television ship is the *Ocean Explorer.* You lie."

"No," Dane said calmly. "We are part of the program, but it is also true that we are operating from the trawler. It's a two-ship operation."

One of the other Russians walked over to Bullet Man and spoke to him softly. Dane wasn't sure why he was worried about volume, since he and Bones couldn't understand their language, but perhaps he was concerned about one of their own hearing? Whatever the case, Bullet's next words gave him pause.

"It is our belief that you are operating on behalf of your government, the *United States* government, in order to keep the capsule's nuclear bomb from becoming a historical embarrassment should its existence become public knowledge."

Dane took a fraction of a second too long to reply.

"Bring them down," Bullet said, nodding to a submariner manning a crane and winch. The sub with Dane and Bones in it was swung away from the watery opening in the submarine's hull and deposited on the floor of what Dane could now see was actually a large airlock. "First you." He swing his AK-47 at Bones. "Out. Slow."

Bones was somehow able to will his sizable form to stand and step out of the sub without lowering his hands. Then the AK's muzzle pivoted to Dane, who did the same. The air here reminded Dane of a Florida swamp in summertime. A rivulet of sweat sluiced down his face as he thought about his Beretta still in his pants, and the ultra-flammable gas now leaking from the submersible's pure oxygen system.

"Remove your knives," Bullet said. Both Dane and Bones removed their dive knives from the sheaths strapped to their calves and slid them across the deck.

"Search them," Bullet said to a pair of muscle-bound shipmates, one of whom approached Dane, the other Bones. The one searching Bones nodded and stepped back, having turned up nothing but a scrap of paper containing a phone number written in flowery, feminine hand.

The man frisking Dane, however, rested his hand on the small of his back; having felt something. He extracted the Beretta and quickly stepped back. Once beyond arm's reach, he opened the clip and closed it again. Then he walked over to Bullet and pressed it into his waiting palm.

"This is necessary for a marine salvor in a deep sea submersible?" Bullet said, pointing Dane's own gun at him.

"No," Dane said quickly, "but I like to have it on the boat to protect from pirates. We are far out to sea in international waters, and I forgot to remove it from my pants before I boarded the sub."

Bullet gave a nod of fake appreciation. "Always so quick with an explanation, you are. Perhaps you have engaged in this line of work before? But I tire of your stories." He uttered a name in Russian and the submariner closest to *Deep Black* went over to the sub.

"Antonov will search your vessel's external holds."

"Your English is pretty good," Bones said. "Where'd you learn it? Sesame Street?"

Bullet looked at him with distaste. "You may direct

your questions to the captain," he replied. "I think he will want to meet you."

Beside him, Antonov opened the sample collection bay that had held the rocks. Frowning, the sailor reached inside and pulled out the small metal box that held the dimes. He handed it off to another sailor who in turn walked it to Bullet. He turned the box over in his hands without opening it. He looked at Dane and Bones.

"What does it contain?" He shook the box, sending up a metallic rattle.

Bones shrugged.

Dane said, "No idea. We just saw it in the capsule and decided to grab it."

Bullet turned the box over once more in his hands. "Too light to be a bomb. I will open it." His scowl said woe betide them if he didn't like what he found inside.

All eyes were on him as he pried up the lid.

"Coins." He scooped a few out and examined them. His gaze turned from interested to puzzled in a heartbeat. "Not valuable." He inspected the dimes inside the box before dumping them out on the floor and then tracing his fingers inside, feeling for a false bottom. He froze, his eyes locked on something on the inside of the lid. He motioned to a crewmember, who stepped forward to look into the box.

"Look here. There are markings of some kind scratched into the lid." He turned an austere gaze to Dane and Bones. "Are you aware of these markings?" Both SEALs shook their heads wordlessly.

Over at the sub, Antonov's eyes grew wide and he

pointed to the hold. Two more crew members trotted over to see what he had found.

"I know for certain you have the bomb on board." Bullet said. "And the captain will want to know all about it. Especially, who sent you to recover it?" He held a hand palm up in front of Dane, who was about to speak. "Please. Say nothing further at this time. Get some rest. We are already underway to take a shore leave. It is good to stretch one's legs on land after so much time at sea, is it not? Breathe the fresh air, clear one's thoughts. There we will discuss things like men."

"Shore leave?" Dane asked.

But the man did not respond. The two newly-arrived crew and Antonov gingerly pulled the nuclear bomb from its hiding place. The three of them walked almost comically over to Bullet in a kind of strange, six-legged dance, their hands forming a collective basket for the powerful device. They set it down at his feet. Bones stole a glance at Dane, who subtly shook his head. *Don't try anything now.*

Bullet seemed not to notice the communication and motioned to two men to his right.

"Show them to their quarters."

Then, to Dane and Bones as they were being led away at gunpoint, he said, "Get some rest while we are en route to our destination."

# CHAPTER 13

**Dane and Bones** looked around at the Spartan submarine quarters they'd been escorted to, a tiny room consisting entirely of cold steel. Bones sat on the lower bunk while Dane occupied a chair in front of a small shelf that served as a desk.

"Not exactly the MGM Grand, but it beats the brig, right?" Bones said.

Dane glanced at the stark metal door. "I'll bet you this *is* the brig." He got up and went to the door. Tried to turn the handle. "Locked."

Bones lay back on the bunk and sighed heavily. "We failed, dude. Russians got the nuke. Got our sub. Got us…"

He wasn't wrong, but Dane remained determined to find a way out of their predicament. "Don't give up. Let's think about it…"

They checked the small room for listening devices and then discussed possible strategies for escape.

"Too bad we don't have a dress and some lipstick." Bones rubbed his chin thoughtfully.

"Why's that?"

"We could put you in drag and let you use your feminine wiles to get us out of here. Who knows how long these guys have been cooped up in this sub with nothing but other dudes to look at? You'd be the belle of the ball."

"If it comes to that, we'll dress you up. You've got the better legs. Now, let's get back to real plans."

They continued to run through their options and speculate about possibilities. Some of the ideas were outright laughable or hopelessly long on odds, but others had at least some merit depending on what situations arose.

They had still reached no consensus on a concrete course of action when they heard a knocking at the door followed by the clicking of a key in the latch. Then the door swung open to reveal Antonov.

"We are near our destination. Please follow me," he said in heavily accented English.

Dane and Bones got up and exited the small space into a narrow hallway with low ceilings made even lower by assemblages of hanging pipework. Caged utility lights lit the corridor while various Cyrillic characters were stenciled on the walls, every inch of this utilitarian space a protest against the idea that humans could not function for extended periods deep beneath the sea.

They stepped through a bulkhead, or "knee-knocker" as the two SEALs knew them from their time aboard U.S. Navy vessels, and continued up a flight of metal stairs to another long hallway. They trooped on in silence, the crewman carrying an automatic rifle slung over one shoulder, walking behind them, but not apparently over-concerned that he would be attacked on the way to wherever it was they were going. At the end of this passageway an open door to the right led into a cramped room with a stair-like ladder leading up. A refreshing breeze wafted from above, and the submarine's motion had a more pronounced rocking to it now.

"This way." Their armed escort nudged his gun barrel up the ladder. Dane and Bones silently climbed a narrow tubular chute from which they could see light spilling down from above.

"Climb up and await further instruction." The guard's voice echoed up through the ladder tube. Dane emerged from the chute in the air, on a high deck platform overlooking the water. After hours spent in the blackness of the deep sea and then the artificially lit underwater world of the Russian submarine, the broad daylight had a blinding effect on him.

Bones cleared the ladder, one hand shielding his eyes. "Now this is a view!" He ignored the two crewmen who had been waiting for them while he took in their new surroundings.

They were docked at the deep end of a long, wooden pier, in aquamarine water clear enough to reveal a sugar-white sand bottom. Sun in the blue sky, calls of seagulls in the air. A palm-studded beach beckoned at the pier's far end.

"Down!" One of the two submariners on the deck waved an automatic weapon in the direction of a boarding ladder. First Dane and then Bones walked to it and descended to the pier.

"I don't usually wear my sweater when I go to Club Med," Bones said, tugging at the uncomfortable garment.

"Remove it if you wish." The nearest guard pointed his gun at Bones while he took off his sweater. Dane slipped out of the jacket he wore. They were glad to leave the heavy garments on the pier.

"What is this place?" Dane asked. All he could see of the land's interior was a patchy wall of palm trees and foliage; not the luxurious tropical growth one would find in a rain forest, but it certainly appeared undeveloped. Large birds wheeled above the thin canopy. A unique ocean scent Dane always associated with low tide tickled his nostrils. Other than the pier, he saw almost no signs of human activity. A derelict oil tanker lay rusting on its side halfway down the beach to their right, trees and vines growing out of its ruptured hull.

Dane's survey was interrupted by four crewmen descending from the sub carrying supply containers. They glared at the two Americans as they passed and proceeded to walk down the pier toward the beach.

"It is an island," one of their two guards said. "The captain will tell you what he wants to about it. Follow those men."

Dane and Bones did as they were told, and for a few minutes there was only the sound of creaking planks as they walked. Upon reaching the beach they stepped onto hot sand and followed the landing party to the left where the beach soon curved out of sight. Looking past the palm trees that marked the edge of the high tide mark, Dane confirmed that the foliage was not thick jungle, but thinner scrub and mangroves that would be penetrable.

Looking back at the sub, it seemed many of the crew were disembarking, some carrying supplies of one kind or another. Dane and Bones continued along the beach, at one point passing other crew returning to the sub, wheeling an empty hand cart.

"This way, stay on the path." Dane's eyes followed the waving gun muzzle to a sandy trail leading through a patch of mangroves. Looking ahead, the path wound over a small rise and across a weed-strewn flatland to a lush patch of trees that partially concealed a two-story house with multiple out-buildings painted in various Caribbean pastels. Dane was mentally debating whether they should attempt a takedown of their guards—once inside the house opportunity for escape would likely be even more limited—when he saw a clump of mangrove trees move in his peripheral vision. He turned his head but saw only still clumps of vegetation.

Dane tripped over a sand-covered mangrove root that sent him sprawling to the ground. Both guards immediately fanned out on either side of the path, one aiming his weapon at Dane while the other covered Bones, who froze in place. As soon as they realized it was an accident and not some kind of escape attempt, they relaxed a little and the group fell back into formation on the trail, walking toward the house. As they neared the complex, a trio of iguanas skittered off the path into the underbrush as the party approached. All three of them were missing their tails completely, yet were still nearly three feet long.

"See you later, stumpy," Bones called, but Dane could only wonder what fate had befallen the animals.

Soon thereafter Bones pointed to a large pile of rocks on the side of the path. "Look familiar?"

Looking at them, Dane noticed their knobby,

porous appearance, and what appeared to be remnants of marine growth. "Hey, those look like…"

"Silence!" One of their guards interrupted, shooting his gun into the sand to underscore the point that there was no one to hear it out here, wherever they were.

Then they came upon a stand of Caribbean Pines that formed a loose circle around the main house—an old, two-story turquoise Victorian affair with a large porch fronting the main entrance. Dane looked but could see no power lines, and guessed that the buzzing he heard in the distance was from a gas-powered generator to supply the house with electricity.

"Up to the porch. Wait there." One of the guards ran ahead to the front door while the other lingered to ensure that Dane and Bones complied. The door to the house opened  and a crew member Dane recognized from the sub held the door open.

"Come in. Dinner is nearly ready."

Dane and Bones stepped into the house's foyer, where a ceiling fan turned lazily over a hardwood floor. Their escort guard wasted no time in closing the door behind them.

"This way." The man who had opened the door led them down a short hallway. Dane caught a brief glimpse of the kitchen, where several of the sub's galley crew were busy preparing the meal, before it broke off to the right into a large, high-ceilinged dining room.

Dane couldn't put his finger on it, but the demeanor of the men seemed somehow off to him. Being in the Navy, he knew firsthand that any kind of shore leave, even if it involved working, was a welcome respite for any sailor. These Russian submariners seemed almost downcast. There was no excited talk, no joking around, no smiles. It almost seemed as though they were happier on board the sub. The only thing Dane could attribute it to was that maybe by stopping here they were extending the duration of their overall mission, when all they wanted to do was go home.

Also odd, Dane noticed, were the bars on the windows. All of them—kitchen, dining room, foyer; even those on the second floor. He supposed it had to do with the fact that months and perhaps even years at a time passed before the captain stopped by, so he needed the security to ward off opportunistic looters.

The sight of the dining table itself pulled Dane back to the purpose of their visit. Dinner. At the center of the room was a long dining table, replete with linen tablecloth, fine china and crystal wine glasses. The captain's chair was at the head of the table, and seated was a broad-shouldered man with steel gray hair and a lined face. His naval officers flanked him on either side. Dane guessed that this was the officer's table. Another long table was also set up in the room, this one occupied by the rank and file. Behind the captain, still armed with his AK-47, Bullet man stood guard, his flinty gaze daring either of them to try anything.

But it was the centerpiece of the captain's dining setup that commanded their attention.

Nested in a basket at the center of his table sat the nuclear bomb.

# CHAPTER 14

**The cylinder stood** less than two feet high, a proliferation of colored wires spewing from each end.

"Please, be seated," the captain said, extending an arm to two open seats closest to him on either side of the table. Clearly it wasn't an invitation but a command, as Dane felt the barrel of their escort's weapon at the small of his back. He hadn't meant to stall. He was simply taking in the incongruous centerpiece, twisted variations on the infamous game of Russian roulette running through his head.

He and Bones took their respective seats. Their plates were already fixed with heaping piles of steaming fish and what looked like fresh salads. A bowl of chowder completed the offering as did a robust glass of white wine.

Bones simply started eating.

The captain chuckled in his direction. "Yes, let us dispense with formalities, shall we?" He himself put his fork to his plate and then the rest of the men around the table seemed to relax and follow suit. The sound of silverware and muted conversation filled the room and soon Dane was able to ignore the nuclear device at the center of the table and eat. He found the food to be delicious and of high quality.

Finally, the captain spoke.

"I assume you have questions."

Dane straightened. "I have several, and you can probably guess what they are: Who are you? What is this place? You know—the obvious ones."

"And what's your chowder recipe?" Bones asked. "I'm seriously considering licking the bowl."

Their host dabbed at his mouth with a cloth napkin before responding. "I am Captain Stanislav Ivkin. We are on my private island retreat in the Bahamas. I bought it years ago for a reasonable sum because it is far from the main islands of commerce and has no water or infrastructure of any kind other than what I myself provided. On the maps it is known as 'Caye Desolation,' but I call it simply, *Mestom Mechty,* which loosely translates in your language to *Place of Dreams* "

Bones made a choking noise mid-sip in his wine.

Ivkin raised an eyebrow. "You disapprove?"

Bones made a dismissive flick with his forefinger. "Don't get me wrong. It's a good-looking chunk of land and I think you and Gilligan would be very happy here, but my dream island would have a few more chicks on it."

Ivkin's expression remained blank.

"And we are here in your dream world because...?" Dane asked. Ivkin's eyes shifted to the nuke on the table.

"I bought this isle personally, not for Russia, a few years ago so that I may have a place to rest while on long voyages to this part of the world. I do not bring the submarine here often, but I think you will agree that it's quite a bit more comfortable here than on board."

"Captain, we noticed a large pile of rocks on the path to the house. We think we've seen their like before. They look like…"

"Like the rocks you saw on the Spanish shipwreck. The ones you so admirably deceived us with?" Ivkin smiled deviously. "We were tracking your submersible on sonar while you visited the wreck."

Dane didn't let this revelation jar him. "Yes. They reminded me of those same rocks. Are they?"

"They are. You see, I located the shipwreck a year before the American television expedition did. I was looking for the space capsule, but became fascinated by the wreck. You know, the crew members are still inside."

Neither Dane nor Bones had a reply for this. They continued to eat until most of the plates were empty or nearly so. The galley crew appeared, clearing the dishes and refilling the wine. When they departed, Ivkin spoke to Dane and Bones.

"Gentlemen, I trust your meal was satisfying?"

Dane and Bones nodded their agreement.

"It's about the only thing that's been satisfying since we've met," Bones said flatly.

"Very well, then. Let us talk about what you Americans would call the proverbial elephant in the room, shall we?"

All eyes went to the nuke.

"What was it doing aboard the space capsule?"

Bones shrugged. "We don't know. We're both a little young to have been involved in that mission."

Ivkin's wolflike grin caused Dane to tense.

"You mean to suggest that you planned a dive on the capsule without knowing of the bomb's existence?" His inflection imparted an air of incredulity to the question.

Bones sipped his wine.

Dane took a moment to make sure that his words would come across not as defensive but matter-of-fact.

"Like my partner said, we weren't even born when the capsule went to space. It's been down there on the bottom for almost forty years. We really had no idea what to expect, and, I suspect, neither does the U.S. government. I think you give them too much credit if you think their record keeping capabilities are that good. If they did have a bomb they probably forgot all about it."

At the other end of the table, one of the Russians who knew English translated for the other men, who erupted in laughter at Dane's remark.

Ivkin tented his hands and looked at Dane while he spoke. "They just forgot all about a nuclear weapon aboard a spaceship, is that it?" An uncomfortable silence befell the table. At length Ivkin asked, "Would you like to hear my interpretation of what happened?" He went on without waiting for a reply.

"I believe that there was another, unpublicized objective for the flight of so-called *Liberty Bell 7*. Did you know that in 1961, in the midst of the Cold War, the U.S. government—your government—had a plan to explode a bomb on the moon as some sort of perverted and vulgar display of space power?"

Recalling Jimmy Letson's words, Dane feigned a look of disbelief, which Ivkin ignored.

"And I can only surmise that something went wrong on that flight. Everyone knows, of course, that the capsule sank after a hatch exploded, but I also believe that something went wrong in space that prevented them from bringing the bomb to the moon. Or, perhaps they never attempted that mission, after all. But the bomb was not there for no reason." He stared at the nuke.

Dane tried to look surprised. "This is also only your conjecture, though. How could you possibly know what happened?"

"You are correct in that I do not actually know. But our intelligence gathering arms run deep. We have long known of the existence of this bomb. In fact, one of NASA's own astronauts was willing to share some information with us before he met a rather untimely end."

Dane flashed on his conversation with Letson, his blood seeming to run as cold as that of the lizard he spotted on a high ceiling beam. .

"But until now," Ivkin continued, "no one was aware of the capsule's final resting place. When the television expedition you claim to be a part of located it, my orders from Moscow came down: collect the atomic weapon and see if we can locate evidence aboard the capsule to show the world the monstrous plans of the congregation of liars known as the U.S. government."

"I still don't see how you can be so certain of what the bomb's purpose was," Dane said, nodding to the cynosure of the table. "How do you know it's not a regular incendiary device that could be remotely detonated to create an underwater sonic signature to aid in recovery efforts should it sink?"

Ivkin laughed. "If that is the case, it did not work very well, did it?" The translator again elicited laughter from the group. Ivkin raised a hand for silence.

"But there is something that I confess I do not understand. Look at the bomb." All eyes went to the cylindrical form.

"Clearly it is intended for dropping through the air. Note how it has the stabilizing fins common to airborne bombs. If it was meant to be deployed on the moon where there is no atmosphere, those fins would make no sense whatsoever. So why put them on?"

"So even you admit that this moon bomb theory makes no sense," Dane said. "Where does that leave us?"

Ivkin shot him a hard stare. "Precisely. So let us try to make some more sense of this, shall we?" He called out in Russian and a crewman appeared at the table carrying the metal box they had retrieved from the capsule. He placed it in front of Ivkin and retreated. Ivkin picked up the box, turned it over in his hands once and then opened it.

Behind Ivkin, Bullet Man spoke up. "As I told you earlier, Captain, I did not inspect the box closely, but I did notice that it has engravings of some sort inside the lid."

"That's the box we retrieved from the capsule. It contained some..." Dane paused. He was not sure what the ramifications of mentioning Roland Streib's involvement with the dimes might be. "...some coins."

"Coins?" Ivkin looked interested. "What happened to them?" He waved a hand over the empty container.

"Ask baldy, there." Bones inclined his head toward Bullet Man. "He's probably been playing dime slots in your casino."

Ivkin frowned and turned his gaze on Bullet Man.

"We did find coins but, because I did not notice anything unusual about them, I did not think them worthy of your attention. I shall have them brought here, though I do not expect you will find anything." He barked a few words in Russian to one of his men, who snapped a salute and hurried away.

Ivkin had returned his attention to the box. "Did you know about the markings?" He turned the box around so that Dane and Bones could see the inside of the lid. They both shook their heads while they stared at a series of dashes and small circles.

"I wonder, could they have any meaning? Seems too orderly to be incidental scratches." Two more of Ivkin's officers got up from their chairs to have a look at the box. They leaned over it, chattering excitedly in Russian for a few seconds until Ivkin spoke.

"Yes, I agree. If we think of the circles not as circles but as dots, then we have the classic pattern of dashes and dots, which, to a submariner is second nature."

Dane's mind instantly clicked with recognition. *Dashes and dots...Morse Code!* Had he given it any thought at all, he'd have recognized the scratches for what they were.

The Russians examining the markings suddenly became excited, calling out for someone.

"My knowledge of Morse Code is, how do you say... rusty? I will have our communications officer examine it," Ivkin said. A few seconds later a squat, black-haired man with beady eyes appeared at his side. Ivkin presented him with the box, pointed to the engravings and then sat back while his officer had a look. After three seconds, the man said something to Ivkin in Russian with an assertive nod.

"As I suspected, it is, in fact Morse Code," Ivkin told Dane and Bones. "It appears that your Gus Grissom had something to say while aboard the spacecraft. Something secret."

"How do we know it wasn't carved into the box before the mission, and he took it along?" Dane posited. "It could just say *Semper Fi* or something like that. Maybe *Carpe diem*!"

"Or *boo yah*!" Bones added.

Ivkin gazed intently at the box as his communications officer produced a pencil and paper and began alternately looking at the box and writing.

"Perhaps. But we are about to find out." Ivkin turned to his communications officer, who had stopped writing. "Golovkin, What does it say? Read it in English for the benefit of our guests."

The officer set his pencil down and picked up the paper. An expression of puzzlement took over his features as he began to read.

# CHAPTER 15

**"Ordered to nuke** Havana. Will abort. Look to LeMay." Golovkin paled as he read.

Ivkin's eyes narrowed dangerously at his officer's words.

"That is the entire message, Captain." Golovkin handed him the written transcription.

"You are certain this is the entire message? No doubts?"

The officer shook his head. "There can be no doubt, Captain. Reading it as Morse, it contains the message I have given you. If it has meaning beyond the Morse, I cannot know it."

Ivkin dismissed the officer, who saluted and returned to his seat.

"Havana! What do you make of it?" he asked Dane and Bones, shaking the paper in his hands.

Dane remained silent. Bones followed his lead. Was this Morse coded box something the Admiral and those who planned their mission knew about? If so they had chosen not to make them privy to it. It wasn't *need to know*. But sitting here as a prisoner on some little known Bahamian outer island, held captive by a Russian submarine captain, it sure seemed to Dane like they could benefit from knowing a little more. Worse, Ivkin seemed to be growing more irate by the second, his face reddening as he re-read the message.

"LeMay...*LeMay*! I know this name..." Ivkin trailed off in thought, his fists clenched, brow furrowed.

Bones looked at Dane with an expression that said, *Who's LeMay*? For his part, Dane had some vague recollection of the name but couldn't place it now.

Ivkin shouted aloud in Russian to no one in particular. When no one answered him, he spoke again, this time in English, looking at Dane and Bones.

"Do you know what this means?"

"No idea," Dane said. Bones shook his head of long hair.

"Curtis LeMay was an American Air Force General, in the early 1960's. He was known for his public clashes over policy with the Kennedy administration."

"You sure do know a lot about American history," Dane observed. "Know your enemy, is that it?"

Ivkin seethed. His voice trembled with rage. "I understand what happened now!" He stood from his chair, sending it sliding backwards over the tile floor, but remained at the table. Dane noticed that he now held a small, smooth rock in his hand that he rubbed like some kind of nervous tic.

"Please enlighten us," Dane glanced at his fellow dining companions, all of whose eyes were riveted to Ivkin. Dane eyed his salad fork, lamenting the fact that steak knives had not been necessary for the meal. He slid the fork up the right sleeve of his shirt, which, after removing his sweater, was simply long underwear. He was grateful for the long sleeves.

Ivkin banged a fist on the table, rattling plates and splashing liquid from glasses. "The Cuban Missile

Crisis of 1962. When it was over, General LeMay requested that he be allowed to bomb Cuba. This despite the fact that Mother Russia had agreed to pull out. He vigorously opposed the naval blockade."

Again, the table was silent save for one of the Russians who knew English translating for his comrades.

Dane was careful to lay his forearm on the table next to his plate before speaking, lest an eagle-eyed observer notice his salad fork was missing. He remembered LeMay now. A hard-liner, or perhaps a whack job, depending on one's perspective. "What's the significance?"

Ivkin's eyes grew wider. "A year earlier, in 1961 during an incident known as the Bay of Pigs, a paramilitary force under the control of the U.S. Central Intelligence Agency invaded Cuba, attempting to overthrow the communist regime. They were unsuccessful."

"So?" Bones said, polishing off his wine.

Ivkin stared at Bones with eyes that seemed full of outright hatred. Bones, even though he was used to people's reactions to his sometimes abrasive outbursts, shrank back in his chair.

"My father, a Russian diplomat at the time assigned to an embassy in Havana, was killed in that invasion when a bomb exploded outside his office. An innocent victim of American imperialism." Ivkin ran his thumb back and forth over the stone.

As soon as the Russian translator completed his sentence the entire room fell eerily quiet. The scrabble of an unknown animal on the roof was the only sound while the sailors seemed to hold their breath.

It was Bones himself who broke the silence. "Sorry about your father, Captain. I grew up without my Dad, too. I know what it's like. It sucks."

Ivkin pressed the heels of his hands hard onto the table as he turned to face Bones. "The message created by Gus Grissom, presumably while aboard *the Liberty Bell 7* space capsule, reads: Ordered to nuke Havana. Will abort. Look to LeMay.' Consider the dates of these historical events."

"The Liberty Bell splashdown was in July of 1961." Dane said.

"Correct. And the Bay of Pigs invasion occurred only three months earlier in April of that same year."

Ivkin pointed at the nuke on the table. "This bomb, carried aboard the spacecraft, was meant to be dropped on Havana, Cuba, but astronaut Gus Grissom refused to carry out his orders, instead landing here." He moved his arm so that it pointed out to the ocean salvage site. "You are familiar with the controversy surrounding the exploding hatch that sank the capsule?"

He looked directly at Dane, his eyes now red-rimmed and bulging.

"Some people say that Grissom blew the hatch early out of panic, causing the capsule to flood."

"Out of panic, yes! That's what he wanted them to think!" Ivkin held up the coded box high and let it fall back to the table with a thud. "But we know now that he was opposed to his mission's secret objective! *Ordered to nuke Havana*! He wanted others to know about his clandestine orders. *Will abort*! And the final piece of the puzzle, "*Look to LeMay*," speaks volumes."

"You're saying the United States ordered Grissom to secretly drop this nuclear bomb on Havana from the space capsule?"

"Yes! It could be done. Cape Canaveral is not all that far from Cuba, especially from a high altitude angled descent from the edge of space. He could have dropped the bomb from the stratosphere soon after his parachute was deployed."

"And this in retaliation for losing the Bay of Pigs conflict?" Dane asked. It disturbed him that he could find no obvious logical flaws in Ivkin's interpretation of the puzzle, even when coupled with what he had been told in the briefing aboard the Lear.

"Yes!" Both of his fists pounded the table along with the word, the flat rock popping out of his right hand and skidding to a stop against Bones' plate The Indian SEAL picked it up while Ivkin continued.

"The CIA was humiliated in their defeat. Castro was still very much in power. Three months later, they saw the spaceflight as an opportunity to unleash total destruction on their enemy. Who would suspect a space capsule delivering a nuclear weapon?"

Bones squinted at the rock, blowing on its surface for a moment as if to clear it of dust, then staring at it again. Ivkin noticed him and extended a hand. "Give that back to me, please. " Bones looked up from the rock and handed it to Ivkin without a word.

"What is it?"

Ivkin scowled at Bones. "It is a good luck charm, if you will, that I have carried for some time."

"So what do you intend to do with this information?" Dane didn't want to spend any more time than necessary in the custody of the Russians. Sometimes he really wished Bones would be quiet, but at the same time he knew the crafty Cherokee was indispensible.

Ivkin eyed the bomb. He spoke in Russian and immediately four of his crew jumped up from the second table and left the room. Then he addressed Dane and Bones.

"I intend to return this bomb to the United States of America."

"So you plan to take this...bomb, if that's in fact what it is," Dane said, "and bring it home with you to Moscow so that they can return it to the U.S. as some sort of public outing of their Cold War plans gone wrong?"

Ivkin spat out a hearty laugh. "Oh, we plan to do a little better than that," he said, pouring water from a crystal decanter.

"Care to elaborate?" Dane asked when Ivkin only drank from his glass, saying nothing further.

"Indeed," Ivkin said, placing his glass on the table."We plan to detonate this bomb ourselves. Justice must be served."

"Out here in the middle of the ocean?" Bones asked. "That would make for some sweet waves. If you've got an extra surfboard, I'm all in."

"No. We are not at war with the Bahamas. You see, we are going to launch it from here, but it will detonate far away, on land. It is time to make preparations."

The four men who left a few minutes ago returned with a cart. They placed the bomb on it and wheeled it away.

"So you're not going to blow up our expedition ships?" Dane tested.

Ivkin stood there with his hands on the table, shaking his head. "Certainly not. We could use our submarine's nuclear warheads for that, even conventional missiles, were that our goal. As I have said, our target is one that will demonstrate to the world that it does not pay to deceive the Soviet Union, and that the true victor of the Cold War is only now coming to light. However, if what you say is correct, that this device is not in fact a nuclear weapon, or has been rendered inoperable from its time on the ocean floor, then the target will suffer considerably less damage."

"And what is the target?" Dane asked.

"None other than Washington, D.C."

# CHAPTER 16

**"D.C. From here?"** Dane asked Ivkin. Only Dane and Bones, Ivkin and two of his crew, no doubt serving as security guards, remained in the dining room.

"Yes, we are at the limit of our range but I believe it to be feasible."

Dane wondered how much damage the small weapon of mass destruction would do in a populated city. He wasn't sure, but if it was supposed to bring Havana to its knees then its power must be significant. And then there were the lingering effects of radioactivity...

Bones jolted him out of his gloomy thoughts by asking Ivkin a question. "Do you plan to issue a warning that the city will be bombed?"

"I am afraid that will not be possible," Ivkin said.

Dane threw his hat into the ring. "Will you take responsibility for the bombing?"

Ivkin smiled. "Oh yes! Why do you think you two are still alive? I am not that desperate for dining companions," he said, looking at his remaining officer who spoke English. That man laughed softly, never taking his eyes off of their two prisoners.

"What do we have to do with it?" Dane asked.

"You will serve as witnesses to the event. I believe you were sent here by your government. I confess that I do not know which branch or agency, but it is of no great matter. You were sent to bring back the bomb, but instead, you shall bring back a firsthand account of how I used that very bomb against your leaders. By the time they hear this account, we will long since have returned to our homeland."

"Coward!" Dane accused. "I can't believe the Kremlin would back such a plan."

Ivkin glared at him ever so slightly and then nodded to his two crew serving as security. They lifted rifles in Dane and Bones' direction. "Perhaps I no longer care what the Kremlin thinks. After all, they were not overly concerned with my father's death in their service. But I will do them this last favor and retire here on my little piece of paradise," he finished with a laugh, rubbing the stone.

"You think we'll let that happen?" Bones said. "We'll make sure the full force of the United States Armed Forces comes down on you like a hammer. Pun intended."

Dane could have kicked him.

"Perhaps you are correct," Ivkin said. "I shall have to find a more permanent solution for the two of you, but I can decide that later. I want you to live to see me exact justice on my father's behalf. Now, let us begin!"

"Now?" Dane asked. "You're going to fire a nuclear weapon on Washington, D.C. right now?"

"What better time?"

"How about never?" Bones suggested.

"You're making a mistake," Dane said. "That old thing probably doesn't work anymore, anyway, and you'll just blow yourselves up." He hoped a dose of fear tactics might scare some sense into the crazed

Russian.

"The nuclear device is relatively simple, being so old, and has already been primed by our nuclear technicians. During its flight to Washington, its reaction will be carried out and reach critical mass, causing a true nuclear blast upon impact. Even if that fails, the primer explosives will cause a conventional explosion that will release radioactive material. Either way, we are about to write our own postscript to a chapter of history the world thought was over." Ivkin nodded to his security detail and they approached the prisoners.

"While my engineers are making the modifications to our missile firing systems in order to deliver the bomb to Washington, you will wait in your quarters, here in the house. I assure you it's much more comfortable than the one aboard my submarine. When it is time, you will be escorted to the submarine to witness this historic event."

**"Well, he was** right," Bones said, resting on a velour couch. "The sub quarters makes this room look like The Ritz."

Dane looked around at their second floor prison. Yellow carpet and drapes, pictures of seascapes adorning the walls, an old rolltop desk against one wall and a four-poster bed in the center of the room. There were windows on two walls, both barred on the outside.

"We must have gotten the guest room."

"Just stay on your half of the bed and we'll be fine,"

Bones said.

"I'm thinking, Bones, that maybe sticking around isn't such a good idea." Dane walked to the nearest of the two windows and peered outside.

"You say that as if we have a choice. There's a trigger-happy Russkie right outside our door, you know."

"But apparently none outside this window." Dane strode across the room to the other window and looked out. "Or this one, but from here I have a view of the path we came in on, and some of the crew heading back to the sub."

He walked back to the first window. He opened it, tensing when the wood creaked at first, then removed its screen. He examined the bars while he listened to Bones.

"Even if we did get out, then what? We're stranded on some little island and our sub is inside their sub, like one of those Russian nested doll sets. We'd have no way to get anywhere."

Dane tested the strength of the bars by pushing on them. Little puffs of plaster fell into the air where the bars attached to the wall.

"I think our best bet is to hide in plain sight. While they're busy re-boarding the sub and preoccupied with the nuke launch preparations, we sneak aboard and hide somewhere. Then, we either wait until they stop in port next and sneak off, or..."

"We hightail it out of there in *Deep Black*!"

"*Deep Black* is an oxygen bomb waiting to happen, remember?" Dane walked over to the desk.

"Well, this is all academic, anyhow, since we can't

get out of…"

Bones broke off mid-sentence when he heard a dull thud as Dane pulled a metal roller track from one of the desk drawers and brought it to the window. Using the flat end of it like a screwdriver, he held it outside the window and started turning one of six screws fastening the grate to the window frame. After a few turns he was able to pull the corner of the grate from the wall. It made a sawing noise as it separated from the exterior wall, and they froze, looking to the door. But their guard hadn't heard it, so Dane resumed undoing the screws while Bones kept a sharp watch on the door, eyeballing the sliver of light where it met the floor.

Once Dane got the rest of the screws out Bones helped him to ease the grate away from the window and tossed it to the dirt below, off to one side so that they wouldn't land on it. They shrunk back from the window while they waited to see if someone would come to investigate outside. When no one did, they looked out the unobstructed window.

Bones shook his head. "This is not the room you wanted as a teenager so you could sneak out at night." Indeed, there was no roof to step out onto but only a sheer vertical drop to the ground about twenty feet below.

"Hang and drop. We can do it." Dane climbed onto the frame, grabbed onto the sill and turned around.

"Go, I hear something in the hall!" Bones warned. Dane let himself drop. By the time the sound of his impact with the ground reached Bones' ears, the large Indian was already falling through the air himself.

He hit the ground next to Dane's impromptu screwdriver. Picking up the piece of metal, he ran, following Dane toward the foliage that bordered the path. Stealthy movement was second nature to the SEALs, and in two minutes they were ensconced in vegetation that afforded them glimpses of the path they'd walked in on. They watched a small contingent of Russians walk past carrying a pair of crates. Looking down the path toward the house, two more submariners walked side by side, each carrying a heavy box.

"We take these two down and put on their uniforms," Dane whispered. In response, Bones smacked the metal bar against his palm and adjusted his footing in the loose dirt. Dane looked up and down the path, saw it was clear except for their two targets.

"I'll take the big guy," Bones said.

"Go!"

Dane and Bones crept silently from the vegetation onto the path behind their intended victims. Bones approached the larger man, on the right, with the metal bar at the ready. Dane ran up to the one on the left. Just as the man turned around at the sound of footsteps, Dane snapped a crisp punch to his chin, sending him stumbling backward. Dane rode him to the ground, slamming the man's head to the ground with a sickening crack.

The Russian lay unconscious, blood from his broken nose pooling in the dirt.

Bones had the taller man in a chokehold with the

piece of metal across his neck. He was on his knees, clawing at the metal bar while gasping and wheezing. Dane assisted Bones by holding down the man's arms and soon he, too, was unconscious.

The two operators dragged the fallen submariners off the path into the brush. Hands patted down the bodies, but besides the uniforms themselves, nothing of value was found.

"Would have been nice to have a gun," Bones lamented, pulling the sailor's jumpsuit from the unconscious man.

"A radio, too. Looks like we got the kitchen runners, though," he said, opening the coolers they carried to reveal leftover food and cooking supplies. Dane changed into the Russian uniform and balled up his clothing, looking around for a place to hide it.

Bones struggled to fit into the uniform he had appropriated, but it eventually fit.

"You look like you're part of the Village People," Dane said. He pointed at something a few feet away before Bones could respond. "There's a hole big enough to stash our clothes."

Bones looked, a concerned expression overtaking his features. "Hole? That's damn near a small cave."

The ground sloped down to a greenery-shrouded depression, and there at the bottom lay a large hole or perhaps tunnel, large enough for a man to wriggle into. A few feet in, it either ended or bent out of sight in darkness.

"C'mon, let's get a move on." Dane took his clothes and slid down to the hole. He tossed his clothing inside, then turned around. "Bones, toss me yours."

Bones knelt on the ground, clothes clutched in one hand, eyes widening.

"*Bones*, throw me…"

Dane froze. Down in the hole, something moved.

# CHAPTER 17

**Bones kept his** voice at a low level. "What the hell *is* that?"

Dane turned back around to look into the hole. He recoiled at the sight of a large animal of some kind emerging from the hole. He scrambled back up toward Bones, but the creature was faster. It dragged itself out of the hole. Dane saw flashes of its jointed legs, five-foot long antennae, and a massive pincer claw that looked as though it would be at home on the business end of a piece of heavy machinery.

"It's a crab!" Dane fell to the ground. Bones reached down to pull him up but it was too late. The humongous arthropod was on Dane in a flash, kicking Bones aside with a sweep of one of its legs. Dane looked up from the ground in time to see a plethora of moving parts he forgot the names of long ago in biology class—mandibles and various other feeding appendages—all moving independently like precision parts of a powerful machine. Something fell from the crab's mouth and landed on Dane's chest—a knobby rock like those in the nearby pile, but dripping with slime.

Dane felt a piece of metal against his wrist and remembered the fork. He pulled it out and jammed the tines deep into the one of the creature's eye stalks. It had little effect. The crab used its legs to pin Dane to the ground. He rocked back and jammed both of his feet into the crab's underside. The animal was jolted just high enough for Dane to roll out from under it…

…only to see another crab scamper out of the tunnel.

"Giant land crab nest!" Bones walked up to the monster nearest Dane and stabbed it with his metal shank. It pierced the creature's hard exoskeleton but sank into nothing.

Bones wrenched the tool out from the creature's natural armor. "It's like punching through drywall. There's nothing on the other side," he shouted. Somewhere in the back of his mind Dane registered that they were being too loud, but he preferred being captured by the Russians if they would save him from these hellish beasts.

Or would Ivkin allow them to be consumed? *Maybe that's why the room wasn't so heavily guarded?*

But he had no time to dwell on such matters. Bones was staving off the first crab with repeated shankings, searching for a vulnerable spot, but the second announced its arrival by crushing Dane's calf in a vice grip with its main pincer. Dane gritted his teeth in pain as he felt warm liquid ooze onto the leg of his Russian jumpsuit. He clutched a fistful of sand and pebbles and flung it into the crab's mouth and eye area. The pincer relaxed its grip ever so slightly and Dane ripped his leg free. He rolled off to one side and stood, not caring if the Russians spotted him.

What he saw terrified him: perhaps a dozen, maybe more, of the land crabs scuttled across the path and through the underbrush, converging on their location.

"Bones, there's more! A whole herd coming."

Bones had picked up a plastic cooler the Russians were carrying and was using it as a shield against the first crab. "Open to suggestions!"

Dane scanned the route they would need to take from here to the sub if they were to remain unseen by the Russians. It was crawling with oversized arthropods, some of them basking on the mound of radioactive rocks, others rampaging across the scrubby undergrowth. The largest ones were taller than Bones. He'd never seen anything like it, but had no time to ponder the miracles of nature. He glanced at the dumped contents of Bones' cooler but it was only a few sacks of flour and some butter. Out of the corner of one eye he spotted the second food box from the Russian he had taken down. He sprinted to it and kicked it over, spilling its contents.

*Yes!* Food. Even better, it appeared to be partially frozen fish as well as some uneaten clams. He dumped out the box and started hurling chunks of seafood off to the other side of the path, away from their needed course. First one crab veered to the offering, then another, then more. It was working. With the exception of the two crabs already battling them, the ginormous crustaceans made for the decoy meal.

Dane glanced over at Bones, who looked like he was at a tipping point in his contest with his ten-legged opponent. "Things are so damn strong," he grunted, struggling to move one of its spindly limbs off his chest with both hands. Dane put his head down and barreled into the meaty decapod. It tumbled onto its back down the incline to the tunnel, where it collided with the other crab, their legs entangling.

"Over here!" Dane pointed through the foliage toward the pier. He threw the last piece of fish out onto the path, baiting three more crabs, then took off at a sprint. Bones was close behind. They passed clusters of land crabs, all either gorging on or fighting over pieces of meat.

They emerged out of the scrub into a patch of sandy soil that soon gave way to a stand of mangroves. The two SEALs flung themselves headlong into the trees, grateful for the cover of the aquatic canopy. Behind them a wayward crab attempted to follow but was too sizable to fit through the tangled, woody growth.

"Keep going." Dane brushed branches out of the way, slogging through wet muck. He worried about losing a shoe. Bare feet were not permitted aboard a naval sub and would make them stand out. He had to slow himself in order to extract his foot with shoe attached on several occasions.

They crashed through the muggy mangrove jungle, wiping spider webs from their faces and slicing their hands on the sharp oysters that clung to the low hanging branches. Bones in particular had a rough time due to his height, but the dogged Cherokee willed himself through the green-and-brown maze until they reached the beach on the other side.

Bones stole a glance over his shoulder. "It's a shame, really."

"What is?"

"I'm just thinking of all the crab claws and deviled

crab we missed out on by not bringing a couple of those things with us."

"Tell you what. We get out of this alive, maybe we'll come back one day and do some crabbing."

Dane and Bones lay at the edge of the sand and surveyed the beach. They watched for the presence of roving guards or patrols, which would indicate that their escape had been noticed. Thankfully, they saw only the orderly, and thinning, procession of Russian sailors boarding their vessel.

"We've got to get on the sub soon, before they notice we're missing." Dane did his best to dry the ends of his pants in the warm sand and soak up some of the blood from his crab wound. Bones was already scratching at the numerous mosquito bites he received in the mangroves. He tied his long hair in a tight ponytail which he tucked down the back of his shirt.

They stood and walked diagonally across the beach, toward the pier, taking a casual approach. If they were being observed from a distance, they wanted to appear like a couple of Russian sailors taking a smoke break, perhaps, or taking a leak before having to re-board the sub.

By the time they reached the pier, they counted only four sailors outside the sub, and these were busy wrangling crates into a cargo net to be lifted to the sub's conning tower.

Dane and Bones kept their heads down and walked to the gangplank that led to the sub's boarding ladder. Dane climbed up first, not too quickly but like he had every right in the world to be there. Bones went next and then they stood on the deck below the conning tower that led into the bowels of the submarine. One sailor was here, preoccupied with using a wrench on some fixture. He gave the two imposters a casual wave without looking up from his work, and Dane and Bones climbed the conning tower.

Reaching the top, Dane took a last look at the island. From up here he could see the house. Suddenly the front door burst open and a Russian ran out with his machine gun at the ready. He looked rapidly right, left, then right again, before shouting a command.

"Now, Bones!"

Dane and Bones dropped down the chute-like conning tower ladder back into the submarine.

# CHAPTER 18

**"They'll want to** be at sea and at depth to launch the nuke. We need a place to hide until the sub gets underway."

Dane suppressed a wave of panic at the long narrow passageway ahead of them that offered no such shelter. They walked briskly, Dane in the lead, down the tight passageway, stopping once to consult a schematic that depicted a room layout. Though not overly familiar with this Typhoon class sub, their time aboard other subs allowed them to recognize the torpedo room in context. Dane memorized its position relative to other major parts of the ship.

They moved down the passage, their footsteps echoing as they traveled through the sprawling steel tube. Halfway down the passageway a sailor entered from the other end and strode their way. Bones walked close behind Dane to hide his head as much as possible, while Dane kept his head down with a hand on one side of his face like he was scratching an itch. They passed without incident and took a left turn into another even narrower passageway, this one with doors spaced at even intervals on both sides. They had proceeded down most of the length of this passage when Dane stopped at a door marked in Russian but with a diagram of a trash can.

"Trash disposal room." Dane knew from his own

Navy experience aboard subs that large ones like this ejected biodegradable trash in compressed discs at sea, while non-degradable trash was stored aboard for later disposal at port. He doubted Ivkin would want trash dumped on his private island sanctuary. "Let's duck in here."

"Into the garbage chute, flyboy," Bones said.

Dane fixed him with a quizzical look.

"Star Wars? Seriously, Maddock, sometimes I think you're a Philistine."

Dane opened the door and stuck his head inside, listening. It was a small room, the walls lined with metal drums. He didn't see or hear any signs of people. Dane and Bones entered the room and closed the door behind them. The space was chilly and reeked of garbage.

"Our accommodations just keep getting better and better on this trip, Maddock. You really know how to travel in style."

"Remind me to request a refund from my travel agent when I get back."

Dane ducked behind a group of drums and hunkered down. Bones followed suit. Should someone open the door and casually look inside, they would not be visible.

A few minutes passed and then they heard a voice come over the sub's PA system. It was in Russian, but from the sound of it the message was not urgent and Dane guessed it meant they were announcing the intention to get underway shortly.

"Hopefully they're still looking for us on the island," he said.

"And they get eaten by those hideous crabs in the process."

"If we're lucky they think we were eaten by those hideous crabs."

They felt a vibration in the room's wall. "Engines are starting up," Dane said.

Shortly after that the pitch of the vibrations changed. "We're underway. Give it fifteen minutes or so. Once we dive we should make our move."

They were both aware that prior to a submarine diving a general alarm would sound along with a message for all submariners to man their stations. After waiting several more minutes, that alarm notice came. Dane raised himself to a kneeling position.

"Torpedo room," Dane said to Bones. "That's where the nuke will be."

They rose and crept to the trash room entrance. Bones put an ear to it and listened for approaching footsteps. Hearing none, he stepped back and opened the door. They left the smelly hiding place, closed the door behind them and took a right down the passageway toward the torpedo room. They had the sub's walkways to themselves since all sailors were manning stations, but this would also raise suspicions if they were noticed. They increased their pace, as if they might be late reaching their stations.

At the end of the walkway Dane consulted another placard map. "This way." They took off down a gangway to the left. Dane held out a hand when he reached a closed door on the right.

"In here. It'll be crawling with people. Hide or

blend in until we can make our move." Dane pulled open the door, which led into a short hallway open to the torpedo room. Bustling with activity, there had to be at least twenty people inside, although they were highly preoccupied with various technical jobs. Ivkin was yelling at a technician next to a bank of control equipment against the left wall of the room.

And in the center of the space, Dane and Bones saw the atomic bomb on a workbench. It had been fitted with an outer casing as well as an application of some sort of lubricant. An assortment of electronic devices and testing equipment littered the work area next to the nuke. Dane recognized an oscilloscope and a voltage meter, but saw other machines he was not at all familiar with.

"Makes me feel so warm and fuzzy inside to know I'm this close to a forty year-old nuclear bomb being tinkered with by Doctor Dumbass," Bones whispered..

Ivkin continued to make demands in Russian to his torpedo technician, his back turned to Dane and Bones. The crewman animatedly explained something, while Ivkin gestured irritably.

Then a Russian voice over the intercom barked out a single word.

Ivkin started to say something to his technician. He was interrupted by a blaring, high-pitched klaxon alarm that initially froze the crew to attention but in short order sent them scurrying to action. He began yelling in Russian and a crewmember reported to him. Dane wasn't sure what was being said, but whatever it was, Ivkin didn't look pleased. He did notice, however, as did Bones, that no one was paying any attention to the nuke.

Another crew member ran to Ivkin, barraging him with a litany of complaints about whatever technical problem it was that they faced.

Then a different alarm, this one a lower, more buzzing sound, joined in with the klaxon.

Dane and Bones looked at one another. Bones glanced at the bomb, ten feet from them on the workbench, unattended while the crew grappled with the alarms.

Bone's eyes widened a split second before he made his move for the nuclear weapon.

# CHAPTER 19

**Bones lifted the** nuke and tucked it under his arm like a football. Dane scanned the room once, but Ivkin and his nuclear technicians were all preoccupied with multiple system alerts.

Without uttering a word, Bones dashed for the exit while Dane kept a few steps ahead of him, serving as his friend's lead blocker. They reached the end of the room and jumped over the knee knocker into the corridor beyond. Thankfully the hall was clear and they accelerated down the empty stretch.

"To the moon pool!" Dane panted.

"Which way?"

Dane flashed on the spatial observations he'd committed to memory on the way over. "Downstairs at the end, halfway down next hall, turn right. It's not far."

But when they reached the bottom of the stairs they were greeted by two crewmen tandem carrying a hefty length of pipe. Unfortunately for them, this meant their hands were occupied, and Dane had dispatched the one nearest to him with a well-placed chop to the neck. The other attempted to swipe a handheld radio from his belt but Dane head-butted him into the steel wall and knocked him out.

"They have weapons?" Bones said, breathing heavily.

Dane frisked them but his hands came away empty. "Keep going!"

As soon as they were underway they heard angry shouts behind them followed by the trammel of footfalls. "Go, go!" Dane encouraged. He could feel Bones' hand on his back as the stout Cherokee pushed forward with the bomb.

They suddenly found themselves face-to-face with Bullet Man. The surprised Russian didn't get his AK-47 raised before Dane barreled into him, batting the weapon to the side and bearing him to the ground. Bullet's breath left him in a rush, and Dane struck the man twice on the temple. The Russian went limp.

Dane scrambled to his feet, snatched up the AK-47, and fired a warning burst toward the sound of pursuit. "That'll make them think twice."

They resumed their  flight, reached the midway point of the tunnel-like corridor, and made the right turn Dane remembered into a short corridor that led to the airlock. Dane sprinted ahead here, for opening the airlock required two hands to turn a large valve wheel. He dropped the AK-47 and threw his body into the effort, thankful that the Russians maintained it well with a regular application of grease. It took some force but opened without so much as a squeak. He immediately went to work on the second airlock door—the one that opened to the moon pool itself.

"C'mon!" Bones said. They could hear the voices of their pursuers, not far behind now, down the passageway they had just left. Dane got the second airlock open and Bones high-stepped through into the moon pool. The cacophony of the systems alarms faded behind them.

"Go to the Russian submersible." Dane grabbed theAK-47 and emptied it at the figures that appeared in the distance. The Russians fell back and Dane slammed shut the outer airlock door and sealed it closed again to slow their pursuers. Then he jumped out into the moon pool area and shut the inner airlock door in the same fashion.

Bones was now passing *Deep Black* as he lugged his hazardous payload toward the Russian submersible that had towed them into the submarine.

"Put the nuke in the Russian sub!" Dane shouted as he ran toward Bones. "Lower it to the pool!"

Bones moved lightning-fast to carry out these tasks while Dane sprinted across the concrete deck, skirting various pieces of equipment and coils of cable and rope. By the time he reached *Deep Black* he could hear the outer airlock door being twisted open.

Dane undid their mini-sub's dome hatch and threw it open. He felt the cool rush of pure oxygen escaping. He snaked an arm inside the sub and found the compartment in which Bones had stashed his Beretta. He fumbled with the clasp for a second, got it, and pulled out the weapon. Comforted by its familiar weight, he spun on a heel, but then stopped. He jumped back into the sub, stooping to access a battery bank. He located the wiring harness and switched the position of two sets of wires, knowing it would cause sparks on ignition.

Dane heard the inner airlock opening. He leapt from the sub back onto the deck. He closed its hatch to leave it as it had been and contain the high oxygen levels inside. He raced over to Bones, who had just lowered the Russian submersible to the surface of the moon pool, where it rocked crazily from its hasty drop.

Dane spotted the nuke lying on the floor of the cockpit on the passenger side. He dropped into the pilot's seat, quickly familiarizing himself with the controls.

"Can you drive this thing?" Bones asked.

"No choice. It's learn or burn. Let's go." He focused his attention on the control panel. His sea gray eyes scowled at the Russian labels. Still, the most important components looked similar to those of the subs he'd just finished training with, and he quickly powered up the deep-sea craft as the angry mob of Russian submariners ran into the moon pool.

Bones jumped into the co-pilot's seat. The agitated outbursts of the approaching Russians were muffled suddenly when Bones pulled the dome hatch down. Dane vented the air in the buoyancy tubes, and their appropriated sub began to sink.

"Wait. I can't find the hatch latch!" Bones was used to the latch from *Deep Black* being on his right side, but it wasn't there. They heard the ping of a bullet ricochet off something close by.

"Bones, no time. We're going down. Just hold the hatch down hard and pretty soon the water pressure will seal it off." Dane felt this was true in theory, although he wasn't looking forward to testing it out.

Bones held onto the hatch's grab handle and then he saw it. "It's in the back. What kind of ass-backwards..." He didn't bother completing the sentence as he reached behind his seat to snap the latch. "Done!"

"Down we go." The last thing Dane saw before he activated the vertical thrusters was a harried crewmember opening the hatch to *Deep Black*. He and Bones watched the moon pool opening fade from view as they absconded into the black void with the Cold War relic.

"We made it, bro!" Bones cheered. "I can't..."

"Not yet, Bones." Dane turned the sub so that they pointed into open water. Then he put the horizontal thrusters on high to propel them out from under the massive submarine.

"What?"

"I want to be far enough away before..."

Suddenly they heard a dull boom and felt a concussive blast rock their little submersible.

"...Deep Black blows." Dane finished, hands roaming the controls to wrangle the mini-sub back to an even keel.

Bones grinned in spite of looking a little pale. "Nice, man. Now they can't follow us except in the mothership."

"Yeah, and hopefully our little oxygen bomb started a nice fire in there that will keep them busy for a while."

"Back to the trawler."

"Hell yes. We've got what we need. Let's go home."

At that moment they heard an alarm sound in the tiny cabin. They'd never heard one before except in simulations and supervised training dives when they'd been triggered intentionally.

"What's up?" Bones asked, looking over at his pilot.

"Uh-oh."

"Maddock! 'Uh-oh' is not something you say in a sub with an alarm going off two miles underwater, man."

"Okay, I take it back, then.

"So what is it?"

"We're low on oxygen and battery power."

"Uh-oh."

"Yeah. Makes sense though, since this thing just got back from the capsule dive to bring us into the submarine, and I don't even think they had it charging at all. They were all focused on us and the nuke."

"I didn't have to unplug any charging cables."

"Nor did they have a chance to swap out the oh-two tanks for fresh ones. Probably not the carbon dioxide scrubbers, either."

Bones took a deep breath and exhaled slowly. "I guess we should have just high-tailed it outta there in our own sub. We had the go-juice and the breathing gas, and they wouldn't have been able to follow us very far in this thing."

"But then we wouldn't have had the explosion, which is what's keeping the Typhoon sub from just blowing us out of the water with a torpedo right now."

"Hey, well that's good news." Bones alternated holding one hand higher than the other. "Air...not blown up...air...not blown up..."

"Speaking of air, maybe we should conserve what little we have left by not talking except when absolutely necessary. I'm going to drop the ballast and aim straight up with the thrusters."

"Do it. The Typhoon's holding position. They're not coming after us. Yet."

Dane dropped the weights the sub carried and put the submersible into a steep powered ascent. They began to rise rapidly toward the surface. Bones called out their depth at significant intervals.

"Two thousand meters..."

Minutes passed in silence where the SEAL duo monitored their equipment and displays. It soon became apparent that it was becoming harder to breathe.

"Fifteen hundred meters...Are we going to lose battery power first or air?"

Dane consulted his gauges, face lined with worry.

"Probably air."

# CHAPTER 20

**Dane tried not** to let the headache interfere with his focus. But as the oxygen levels in the sub dropped and carbon dioxide increased, he was all too well aware that the throbbing pain in his temples was going to get worse before it got better. He looked over and saw Bones glance at the depth meter before closing his eyes and rubbing his temples.

"One thousand meters…" he announced without enthusiasm.

"Just about a half mile to go," Dane said. "We'll make it." He tried to sound confident. At least he took comfort in the fact that the water outside their protective sphere was now only black as opposed to pitch black. And looking up, he was pretty sure he could see some gray. Their rate of ascent was increasing, too, although that also meant less control over the sub's trajectory.

"Vertical thrusters on high," he informed Bones. Eyeing the compass, he kept the submersible pointed in the direction of their trawler.

Bones glanced at their sonar, which thankfully showed an empty screen. The Russian sub was not yet in pursuit. He knew that a missile could show itself on the monitor, though, for a few seconds before it slammed into them, ending their existence in a single muffled implosion. He was about to voice this concern to Dane when the comforting hum of the sub's thruster motors stopped. Silence. The cabin lights and instrument displays flickered for a moment, then came back on.

"We lost main battery power," Dane said, almost panting now. "Reserve kicked on but it's only got enough juice to run the oh-two pumps and the cabin lights."

Bones studied their depth gauge. "We're still rising. 500 meters. I can see light up there," he said, plastering his face to the acrylic dome while he gazed toward the distant sky.

And then the cabin lights blinked out.

Dane and Bones looked around in the near darkness. The constellation of LEDs and various indicator lights that normally lit up the inside of the sub had been extinguished. Bones waved his hand in front of his face and could barely discern it. Most worrisome of all, their rate of ascent had begun to slow.

"Are we sinking?" Bones voiced their worst fear: plummeting back into the abyss as helpless as a stone, where they would suffocate on the bottom in their acrylic tomb. "No more depth gauge readout."

Dane stared in vain out through the sub's spherical window. With no reference points to look at, he couldn't tell if they were rising, falling, or maintaining position. "Can't say. I can dump the rest of our ballast, though."

"Do it."

It was the closest thing to fear in Bones' voice that Dane had ever heard. Glad for the fact that the ballast dump was a mechanical system and therefore not dependent upon battery power, he pulled a lever that opened a flap in the buoyancy tubes, releasing hundreds of pounds of lead shot. "There they go."

"Hopefully they land on Ivkin's submarine down there," Bones said. In spite of the situation, Dane laughed. "Clog up the missile tubes, right?"

Bones started to laugh then forced himself to quit. "Stop it, man. We don't have the air for that."

They could only stare outside their bubble and wait. After a couple of minutes their eyes had adjusted to the low light conditions, and it soon became clear that they were in fact still rising.

"Getting lighter," Bones rasped. He craned his neck to look upward, where he saw only a dimensionless, whitish haze.

Dane reached down toward the floor of the cabin. "No mechanical override for the rudder's joystick. We're going straight up, which means we'll probably come up short of the boat."

"I don't care where we come up," Bones gasped, "as long as we come up."

Dane did not want to vocalize his thoughts. Looking up, he could see that it was definitely getting lighter, but they were perilously close to going unconscious. Peering out the dome, his heart spiked with hope as he saw a school of silver fish dart overhead, their white bellies flashing as they turned. They had left the deep sea zone behind and entered the upper layers of the ocean, the realm where scuba divers could venture.

"I see fish, Bones. Hang in there." But he heard no

response from his fellow SEAL. Bones kept nodding off.

"Bones! Don't go to sleep, buddy, c'mon!" He gave him a shove.

"Huh...what?"

"Wake up, man! Dane's voice was at a near whisper. "Almost there." He pointed up.

Bones supported his head against the cabin dome. Dane's urge for oxygen was painful now, and he entertained thoughts of throwing the dome hatch open and making a mad dash swim for the surface. Deep down he knew that even if he wanted to try that—or needed to, if the sub began to sink instead of rise—that the water pressure even at shallow depths would prevent them from pushing it open while underwater.

Minutes passed in a haze of shallow breathing. Dane's headache made it difficult to think straight and Bones hadn't said anything in a while. He occupied himself by trying to start the dashboard controls; he knew that sometimes batteries would build up a reserve charge after they rested, but now he was having no luck. Then he gazed up through the dome, and there it was.

The surface!

The shimmering underside of the waves sparkled and danced above their rising sub.

"Bones. Bones! Get ready."

"What?" he whispered without moving.

"One hundred feet! Let's get ready to crack this hatch as soon as we surface." The Indian SEAL remained motionless.

Dane saw a sea turtle fly by their window and he

could tell that their little sub was moving fast. "Hold on, Bones. We're gonna pop on out like a champagne cork and splash back down."

He moved his friend's hand to a handhold and was relieved to feel Bones grip down on it. He could see his face now and was reassured by the fact that his eyes were open.

Another quick glance at the surface told Dane that they were maybe fifty feet away and closing at some scary feet-per-second rate that would have made their sub instructors furious.

He did not have the breath to put air behind it, but he mouthed the words, "Here we go…"

The Russian mini-sub burst through the sea surface into the realm of sunlight and air. The world was a chaotic swirl of blue sky, water, and a ball of sun. Dane saw the form of their trawler perhaps fifty yards from them, bobbing serenely on the surface.

Unbelievably to Dane, Bones instantly scrambled to life and went for the latch that would open the hatch and deliver them sweet air.

"Wait!" Dane rasped, but it was too late. Bones could no more be stopped from opening that hatch even though their sub was now airborne than a starving dog could restrain itself from gobbling down a bloody steak dropped in front of its nose. Bones leaned over the seat and Dane heard a clicking noise. Immediately he felt the rush of cool air.

Then the sub reached the apex of its airborne arc and began to fall back to the ocean. It canted over and splashed down on Dane's side, drenching him with water as the sea invaded their cockpit. They'd landed almost upside-down and with the hatch open. Dane knew from his training that usually this type of situation was the result of a botched sub launch. But regardless of the cause, he was all too aware that it was a potentially deadly position that he had been trained to avoid at all costs.

His feet sloshed in water as he turned to Bones. "We gotta get out. Now!" Bones made a move to grip the edge of the sub and nearly lost the fingers of his right hand when the dome hatch came slamming back down under the force of the water currents. He withdrew his hand just in time. Then the hatch opened again, closing and opening like an angry clam as they drifted.

Dane didn't see how they would escape without injury. But the water was up to his waist now, so he was preparing to take his chances when suddenly Bones reached down to the cabin floor.

"Bones, you okay?"

He could see the strain on Bones' face, and then the nuke appeared in his lap as he lifted its weight from the floor. "Help me," he said, hefting the bomb up toward the rim of the sub's cabin. Dane moved over to the co-pilot's seat and together they wrangled the heavy device onto the edge of the cabin such that it prevented the hatch from closing all the way.

Water swirled about their shoulders.

"Go, Bones. Slip through!"

Bones stared wide-eyed for a second at the hazardous cylinder propping the flapping dome open, then squirmed out through the slim space into the ocean. Once through, he treaded water, holding the bomb in position while Dane squirmed through after him.

Dane looked around. The TV expedition's *Ocean Explorer* was in the same spot, looking busy with their salvage operation. Much closer by was their trawler. He saw no other activity. Their mini-sub was rapidly filling with water and would soon sink back into the depths from whence it came. Dane knew that even in their weakened condition, he and Bones would be able to make the swim back to their boat. Their BUDS school experiences had seen to that. That wasn't the problem.

He eyed the nuke, still wedged in between the sub's frame and the dome hatch. It was far too heavy for even both of them to tread water with. The thought of losing it now after all they had been through nearly made him sick.

"Bones. We need to get the bomb."

# CHAPTER 21

**"Bomb's way too** heavy to swim with," Bones sputtered, still weak from his ordeal in the oxygen-depleted submersible.

"I know," Dane said, eyeing their boat about two hundred feet away. With the trawler's autopilot system maintaining a fixed position, he and Bones were drifting in the opposite direction from the boat. He knew they had to do something, and fast. There had to be a way to float the nuke…

Dane peered inside the rapidly flooding cabin. *Submersible, flotation…buoyancy…*He mentally ticked through all of the sub's systems and still came up empty on how to use them to save the nuke. Then the sub wobbled precariously, and he saw it: a snatch of orange behind the seats.

Life jackets!

Like all seagoing vessels, even submersibles were required to carry them aboard. Dane gripped Bones' shoulder.

"I see PFDs inside. Going in." Before Bones could reply Dane took a deep breath and squiggled though the hatch held open by the nuke. Inside the cabin his head was underwater. He opened his eyes to a blurry cockpit and the sting of saltwater. He pulled himself by feel back to the seat where he'd seen the life preservers. The sub knocked over to the right once and he had to reorient himself. Then he saw the blurry patch of orange and reached a hand out. He yanked on it but it stuck, secured in place by some kind of restraint. He slid a hand along the front of it and located a clasp. He undid it, pulled again, and a personal flotation device came free.

He swam up so that he could put his head up to the dome in the hopes of securing a breath. He managed a half gulp of air before the entire cabin gave in to the ocean.

*Sub's flooded!*

Any second now, the underwater craft would succumb to the depths.

Dane returned to the PFD area and saw the remaining blotch of safety orange. He reached out and grabbed this one, which he liberated. Both PFDs in tow, Dane pulled himself back over to the open hatch, where he was relieved to see the nuke still in place, Bones' hands supporting it from outside. He slithered back through the open hatch, the dome bruising his lower back on the way out.

Outside the sub treading water next to Bones, Dane wrapped the first life jacket around the nuke and cinched it down tight with the straps. By the time he finished the sub was four feet underwater.

"Better grab it," Bones cautioned.

"Let's go," Dane said signaling with a thumbs-down for Bones to swim under with him. Forcing the PFD under, Dane wrestled it down to the sub and managed to tie it to the first PFD. Then he saw Bones strong-arm the nuke out from under the hatch. Dane clutched the nuke also and the two SEALs kicked back up to the surface.

Even with both PFDs attached to the nuke, it still wanted to sink. But with both Dane and Bones gripping the bomb and kicking, they could just manage to keep it afloat.

"The boat," Dane coughed, nodding in the direction of their trawler. They began to kick, heads going underwater after each breath they took. But they kept kicking, and when Dane looked up some time later, he saw their boat's stern welcoming them. They swam to a ladder and Dane climbed aboard while Bones cradled the nuke in the water, supported by the ladder. Climbing up with the nuke would be too difficult in their weakened state. Dane searched the work deck and came up with a long, stout rope. He brought it to the stern and dropped it down to Bones, who tied it around the nuke and knotted it.

Dane hauled the nuclear weapon aboard their boat. He and Bones rushed it inside the cover of the lower cabin area where they secured it beneath a pile of fishing gear.

The SEALs high-fived one another. "To the wheelhouse," Dane said.

They ran up the stairs to the cockpit. Inside, Dane quickly took out the satellite phone.

He lit the thing up and dialed the number Epson had made them commit to memory. As instructed, when the line opened he input their latitude and longitude coordinates, followed by their speed and heading. He heard a synthesized voice: "Your information has been recorded," and then the line went dead.

"Do we sit and wait knowing the Russians could blow us out of the water any second or get out of here under our own power even though it'll change our position?" Bones asked.

In answer, Dane disengaged the auto-pilot and flipped the hidden switch to activate the secret twin engines. He set them on a course due east at full throttle.

As they left the site, they looked over at the *Ocean Explorer*, where an arresting sight awaited them.

Suspended by an A-frame crane, the space capsule *Liberty Bell 7* dripped water onto the ship's deck.

"He did it." Bones said. "Roland Streib, that crazy bastard."

"I hope he decodes his dimes," Dane said with a grin.

"I'm sure he'll come up with a great hidden message for them."

"As long as Jimmy was right and it doesn't say, 'Don't forget the nuke', we're all good."

Bones opened a window to the wheelhouse and gazed out across the waves. "So weird," he said, contemplating.

"What's that?"

"A sixteenth century Spanish treasure ship carrying radioactive ore sinks right here, on the same spot that a nuclear bomb sank in a spacecraft four centuries later."

Dane nodded as he also stared out over the open sea while their vessel plowed toward the  Florida coast. "It all worked out pretty good. We completed our mission. The Admiral gets his A-bomb. Streib gets his capsule."

"We got to destroy two mini-subs!"

"Right, so I was thinking about that. Not sure how happy they'll be about us leaving *Deep Black* with the Russians. But it was just you and me out here, on this Top Secret mission. That means we get to write the history here, Bones. So how do we explain coming back with the nuke but without the submersible?"

Bones gazed out across the silver-colored sea. "Chalk up another one for the Bermuda Triangle."

## *-The End-*

# ABOUT THE AUTHORS

David Wood is the author of the popular action-adventure series, The Dane Maddock Adventures, as well as several stand-alone works and two series for young adults. Under his David Debord pen name he is the author of the Absent Gods fantasy series. When not writing, he co-hosts the ThrillerCast podcast. David and his family live in Santa Fe, New Mexico. Visit him online at www.davidwoodweb.com.

Rick Chesler is the author of the popular Tara Shores Thriller series and several other thrillers. Rick holds a Bachelor of Science in marine biology and has had a life-long interest in the ocean, its creatures and the people who call it their home. When not at work as a research project manager, he can be found scuba diving or traveling to research his next thriller idea. He currently lives in the Florida Keys with his wife and son. Visit him online at rickchesler.com.

Enjoy this preview of

# LIBERTY

## A DANE AND BONES ORIGINS STORY

By David Wood and Edward G. Talbot

**"On the plus** side, he hasn't tried to shoot us."

Uriah "Bones" Bonebrake wasn't gripping the wheel of the rented Mustang convertible with any more than normal pressure, but his face did betray a small amount of concern. Dane Maddock, the man sitting in the passenger seat, couldn't quite bring himself to chuckle at the joke. They were being followed and he had no idea why.

He turned to Bones while keeping one eye on the rear-view mirror. "I saw that white Ford Taurus at the airport, idling near the rental car pickup. Same driver at the wheel, same red, white and blue USA hat. With all the turns we've taken, there's no way it could be a coincidence having him behind us."

Bones took his eyes off the road for a moment to look at Dane. "What do you mean Taurus? It's the blue Chrysler that's following us."

"It was at the airport?" Dane frowned.

"Yeah, by the cabs. Driver's got a beard that would make ZZ Top jealous."

"You realize we could be imagining things."

"Two cars are at the airport at the same time as us. We drive aimlessly through the city before getting breakfast at a Krispy Kreme, and the same cars are following us when we leave the parking lot. I don't care how good the jelly donuts are, that's no coincidence."

"So we have a blue Chrysler and a white Ford on our tail."

Bones chuckled. "Both American cars. All we need is a red Chevy and it'll be like the fourth of July."

The mention of the fourth of July triggered something at the edge of Dane's thoughts, but he couldn't quite grab hold of it. "So who are they? What do they want?"

"No idea. But them following us offends me."

Bones depressed the accelerator and they shot through the red light where they had been stopped. Dane glanced in the mirror and saw that the Ford had followed but the Chrysler remained stuck as a line of cars started across the intersection in front of it.

"One down, Bones. Halfway there."

"I haven't even broken a sweat yet. For my next trick—"

Bones slammed on the brakes, allowing the car to spin sideways. With a squeal of rubber he flew up a side street. He repeated a similar maneuver three more times at different streets.

"They still there, Maddock?"

Dane looked in the mirror and saw no cars. He risked turning his head all the way around, and for a hundred yards behind them, the street was clear.

"Doesn't look like it."

"Cool. We still gonna check out Independence Hall?"

Dane was amazed at how calm Bones seemed after the maneuvers with the car. Then again, compared to their SEAL training, a few tight turns in traffic hardly merited a yawn. The two had just completed the three week Jump School phase of Navy SEAL training in San Diego and were in Philadelphia for a few days of sightseeing before heading to Boston. In Boston, they would visit Melissa and Courtney, two women he and Bones had first met in Boston just before Jump School. Despite having spent just a few hours together on a single evening, Dane knew Melissa was something special. Soon he'd have an opportunity to get to know her better.

He realized that he was glad to have Bones with him, despite the man's seeming inability to take anything seriously. A Native American six and a half feet tall, Bones cut an imposing figure, but he often exuded the joy of a teenager putting one over on the old folks. On the red-eye flight from San Diego to Philadelphia, Bones had spent most of the time attempting to seduce the first class stewardess. This was after conspicuously traveling in his dress whites to convince the gate agent to upgrade them to first class. Dane could still hear the exchange in his mind.

"I think she likes me."

"Maybe she's a glutton for punishment, Bones"

"Awesome, Maddock made a joke. I told you this trip would be fun. Hey, think she wants to join the mile high club?"

"I'm sure she's never heard that line before."

"Yeah, but this time it's me."

Dane was learning that despite the constant jokes, the big man was rock-solid when things got dangerous. He just hoped the apparent danger they faced now turned out to be nothing.

Five minutes later, they were near the University of Pennsylvania, where three large buildings seeming to rise higher than the rest on campus. It always amazed Dane how the campuses at big universities were like small cities in themselves. He glanced in the mirror one more time, though he hadn't seen anything in his previous checks.

"Bones, they're back! And—" Dane stopped, not believing what he saw.

"What else, dude? Spit it out."

"There's also a red Chevy with them."

**LIBERTY- COMING SUMMER, 2014**

14322500R00112

Made in the USA
San Bernardino, CA
24 August 2014